Dear Reader,

Would a rose by any other name smell as sweet as Rex Brody? He may not quite be the Romeo that Tamara Ledford had always dreamed of, but he reveals himself to be charming in his own cocksure, irresistible way.

Rex Brody was first introduced in my novel *Return to Santa Flores,* and I was so swept away by his audacious spirit and larger-than-life personality that I knew I had to give him stage time come along with her interest in horticulture, and it's easy to understand why Rex is so eager to wake up and smell these particular roses! I hope that you will be enchanted by this unlikely but lovable duo.

Iris Johansen

PRAISE FOR IRIS JOHANSEN

"Iris Johansen knows how to win instant fans."
—Associated Press

"Iris Johansen is a powerful writer."
—*The Atlanta Journal-Constitution*

"[Iris Johansen is] one of the romance genre's
finest treasures."
—*Romantic Times*

"A master among storytellers."
—*Affaire de Coeur*

"Johansen serves up a diverting romance
and plot twists worthy of a mystery novel."
—*Publishers Weekly*

"[Iris] Johansen has . . . a magical quality."
—*Library Journal*

"[Johansen is] a consummate artist who wields her pen
with extraordinary power and grace."
—*Rave Reviews*

"Iris Johansen is a bestselling author for the best reason—
she's a wonderful storyteller."
—CATHERINE COULTER

"Iris Johansen is incomparable."
—TAMI HOAG

BOOKS BY IRIS JOHANSEN

IRIS JOHANSEN

No Red Roses

BANTAM BOOKS
NEW YORK

2013 Bantam Books Mass Market Edition

Copyright © 1984 by Iris Johansen

Published in the United States by Bantam Books, an imprint of The Random House Publishing Group, a division of Random House, Inc., New York.

BANTAM BOOKS and the HOUSE colophon are registered trademarks of Random House, Inc.

Originally published in hardcover in the United States by Bantam Books, an imprint of The Random House Publishing Group, a division of Random House, Inc., in 1984.

ISBN 978-0-345-53959-5
eISBN 978-0-345-53960-1

Cover design: Eileen Carey
Cover photograph © Vladimir Piskunov / Getty Images

Printed in the United States of America

www.bantamdell.com

9 8 7 6 5 4 3 2 1

Bantam Books mass market edition: October 2013

For Tamara

My gypsy who thinks nice
guys are sexier

No Red Roses

ONE

WITH A SIGH of relief, Tamara Ledford pulled into the driveway of the roomy old Victorian house where she'd lived all her twenty-three years. The gracious, turreted white frame house exuded an aura of mellow serenity that seemed to wrap her in a comforting embrace, and she badly needed that comfort at the moment. She jumped out of her old Toyota, slammed the door, and walked swiftly along the flower-bordered path and up the four stairs to the frosted glass-paneled front door.

She paused for a moment and drew a deep breath, trying to cool the anger and tension that had robbed her of her usual composure. There was no sense in disturbing Aunt Elizabeth over something as trivial as Celia Bettencourt's bitchiness. And, if she didn't calm down, her aunt would definitely notice how upset she was. Even if Aunt Elizabeth's "gift" wasn't fully operational at any given moment, like this one, she was always uncannily perceptive.

When Tamara opened the front door, she was immediately enveloped in a deliciously spicy aroma. Gingerbread, she identified with a sudden lift of her spirits, as she quickly made her way down the linoleum-covered hallway to the large old-fashioned kitchen at the back of the house.

Aunt Elizabeth was at the kitchen table spreading white sugar icing on the luscious sweet bread, and she looked up with a quick smile at Tamara's appearance. "Hello, dear. Aren't you home a little early?" she asked absently, as she turned the plate and dipped her spatula once more into the bowl of icing.

"A little. I came home early to dress for Mr. Bettencourt's party," Tamara replied, strolling over to the table and dropping into a gingham-cushioned ladderback chair.

"Oh yes, I'd forgotten that was tonight," Elizabeth Ledford said vaguely. She looked up, her blue eyes suddenly sparkling. "What are you planning on wearing?"

"I haven't decided," Tamara said evasively, then knowing the suggestion that was coming, she went on hurriedly. "I see you have on your Madame Zara outfit." Her violet eyes twinkled. "Who have you been peering into your crystal ball for now?"

Her aunt looked down with serene satisfaction at her midnight blue caftan that was extravagantly embroidered with silver stars and crescent moons. She always claimed the rather bizarre outfit inspired her clients with confidence, despite her great-niece's constant teasing raillery. "Mildred Harris's Pekingese ran away last night. She was most upset."

Tamara dipped a finger into the mixing bowl and scooped a bit of icing off the side. She grimaced, as she slowly licked her finger. "I'd run away too, if I were as smothered with attention as that poor animal. Did you locate him?"

Her aunt shook her head reprovingly. "You should be a little more understanding, Tamara. That Pekingese is the only living creature that Mildred has to care about since her husband died. She can't help it if she goes a bit overboard at times. After all, she *is* getting older."

Tamara smothered a smile at that last remark. Elizabeth Ledford at seventy-three was at least six years older than Mildred Harris, but she never seemed to be conscious of the fact that she might be considered a senior citizen. She certainly didn't look anywhere near her age, Tamara thought idly. Aunt Elizabeth's slim, athletic body was as straight and lively as ever. Her face was as unlined and smooth as a woman of forty, and her sparkling blue eyes were constantly dancing with enthusiasm and humor. Though her hair was snow white, it curled in a riot of tight shiny curls around her face, increasing the aura of youthfulness.

"Sorry," Tamara said solemnly. "Did you find the Peke?"

"Of course," her aunt said serenely. "He got locked in the fruit cellar by mistake when Mildred was fetching some peach preserves. He didn't really run away. When I told Mildred where he was, she hurried right home to let him out."

"I wonder if she'll be able to coax him out. He's probably enjoying his vacation from that eternal fussing," Tamara said with a grin.

She never doubted for an instant that the dog would be exactly where Aunt Elizabeth said he would be. As a child she'd accepted as a matter of course that her aunt could *see* where she'd misplaced her doll or lost her favorite hair ribbon. Aunt Elizabeth had once explained to Tamara that she would break her arm in the next few days, but that she mustn't be frightened and would be quite well again in a few weeks. Tamara hadn't even been surprised when the rope on her swing had broken and she'd had to be rushed to the hospital with a fractured radius.

She'd thought all grownups possessed these powers until she'd started school and been rudely disillusioned. She'd discovered that Aunt

Elizabeth was "different." When a bully called her aunt a witch, Tamara had socked him so hard his nose began to bleed copiously and he'd run crying to the teacher.

Tamara had learned soon, though, that she couldn't fight *all* the kids who taunted her. So she'd come to behave with a cool reserve that had been her armor ever since. She'd cared much more passionately when the other children had hurled insults at Aunt Elizabeth than when they'd jeered at her for her illegitimacy. Aunt Elizabeth, in her infinite wisdom, had prepared her for the latter possibility. But because she'd lived with her own strange powers so long that they'd become second nature, it never occurred to her to warn Tamara against the venom of those who were frightened or skeptical of her gift. For years Tamara had been silently, yet fiercely resentful of the condemnation of her aunt by her peers, until she'd come to realize just how unusual a gift Elizabeth possessed.

Her aunt's blue eyes were keen as she looked up now and smiled gently. "Are you going to tell me now why you really came home early, dear?"

"I told you I had to dress . . ." Tamara's voice trailed off. "Well, it was partly true," she said sheepishly. She ran her hand through her shining blue-black hair and with a rueful shake of her head met her aunt's steady gaze. "I'm just being stupidly emotional over something I should have learned by now to ignore. Celia Bettencourt was a little too much to put up with today." Tamara made a face. "I wish to heaven her father had seen fit to place her in someone else's department to learn the ropes."

Her aunt turned the plate again and started icing the other side of the gingerbread. "It was perfectly natural for him to want her to learn from you," she said calmly. "Every father wants what's best for his children and he knows your Perfume and Herb Boutique is the best run department in his entire chain of department stores."

Tamara knew without vanity that her Aunt Elizabeth was correct in her judgment. Tamara had worked hard enough in the past five years to assure herself of the boutique's success. "I think we'd both be happier if he'd chosen someone else to train her in merchandising," she said gloomily. "We've never gotten along, even as children. And since she came back from finishing school in Switzerland, she's been absolutely impossible. She never misses a chance to take a verbal jab at me."

"Did it ever occur to you that she might be suffering as much as you?" Aunt Elizabeth suggested, her expression thoughtful. "Jealousy can be a terribly disturbing emotion. It can burn you up inside."

"Jealousy?" Tamara looked at her in blank disbelief. "You've got to be kidding. Her father's the richest man in town and Celia is more than aware of how attractive she is."

"Is she?" her aunt asked. "I wonder. You'd be very potent competition for any woman, love." Her gaze ran over her great-niece in affectionate appraisal. "You're very beautiful, you know. You have that wonderfully wicked look I imagine a king's mistress might have." Her gaze returned to her cake. "Besides, you have something I rather think Celia would give a good deal to possess."

"And what is that?" Tamara asked.

"Walter Bettencourt's respect and admiration," her aunt answered quietly. "She knows her father not only trusts your business acumen, but has genuine affection for you. That's a pretty bitter pill to swallow when she probably realizes he doesn't give her the same respect."

"She's the apple of his eye," Tamara protested.

"As a daughter," her aunt said, her face compassionate. "Not as a friend. You have to earn friendship. Maybe that's something Celia doesn't realize yet. Perhaps she thinks you've stolen that from her."

"You're a very frustrating woman to be around, Elizabeth Ledford," Tamara said, her lips curving in a tender smile. "I fully expected to be soothed and cosseted, and you actually have me feeling sorry for the bitch." She scowled as she remembered the extremely trying day she'd just undergone. "And she *is* a bitch, Aunt Elizabeth."

"I don't doubt it for a minute, dear," her aunt said serenely. "I just want you to come to understand *why* she's a bitch." She smiled. "And you don't really need cosseting, do you? It's the Celias of this world who need reassurance and sustenance. You're quite strong enough to face anything, Tamara."

Tamara stood up suddenly and leaned over to kiss her aunt's cheek. "You're pretty terrific! Do you know that, Madame Zara?" she asked huskily, and then before her aunt could answer, she was striding briskly toward the door. "I think I'll change into my gardening clothes and work in the greenhouse before I get ready for the party. Marc won't be picking me up till eight to take me out to dinner." She raised a brow inquiringly. "Have you decided to attend the party?"

Her aunt shook her white curly head. "I don't think so. The vibrations are always so strong in that large a crowd that it invariably gives me a headache. Besides, there's a bingo tournament and a covered-dish supper at the church tonight."

"I'm tempted to skip the party myself." Tamara sighed, making a face. "If I hadn't promised Mr. Bettencourt I'd be there, I think I would skip it. I've had enough of Celia for one day and

I can do without watching her play lady of the manor."

She would just have to avoid Celia this evening. It shouldn't be all that difficult. Walter Bettencourt had invited practically everyone in Somerset, New Hampshire, to celebrate the first anniversary of his marriage to his attractive wife, Margaret. A widower for fifteen years, it had been a nine-day wonder when Bettencourt had attended a convention in New York last May and returned two weeks later with a bride. He obviously was crazy about her, and Tamara could readily understand the reason. Margaret Bettencourt was a charming and intelligent woman who still possessed a glowing attractiveness. Tamara had met her several times when she'd come to the house for consultations with Aunt Elizabeth, and found her both gracious and kind.

"I wonder if there would be room for me in Mildred Harris's fruit cellar? I feel a little like running away myself." Tamara sighed again. "Have a good time, love." She blew her aunt a kiss and hurried out of the kitchen.

Three hours later, Tamara reluctantly put away her spade and trowel, checked the thermostat and humidifier, and turned out the lights in the greenhouse. As usual, the hours spent working so happily in her herb garden had flown by, and she was tempted to spend the evening contentedly puttering with her plants rather than attending that dratted party. She'd always had a passion for horticulture, and she'd had her own herb garden from the time she was six. As a birthday present when Tamara was twenty-one, her aunt had insisted on having a small greenhouse built in the backyard so she could enjoy her hobby year round. It was Tamara's pride and joy, and she spent every free moment there.

Oh well, Marc Hellman was escorting her to the party and she couldn't just stand him up. She'd have to go and try to make the best of it. Marc wasn't the kind of man who would understand any impulsive change of plan. His keen legal mind was respected by everyone in town, but he was so methodical and so pedantic.

As she passed through the kitchen, she noticed it had a pristine emptiness. Aunt Elizabeth must have already left for her church social, she thought absently. However, when she reached her room, she discovered that her great-aunt had left her a note that caused Tamara to shake her head ruefully.

The note was pinned to a crimson taffeta gown that lay like a brilliant poinsettia on the earth-colored coverlet on her bed. It was short and lovingly coercive:

Darling,

I know you want to look your very best to-night, so I pressed this gown for you.

Have a lovely time!

E.

Aunt Elizabeth passionately hated Tamara's wardrobe, which she described as dull and mouselike. She'd given Tamara this lovely creation last Christmas, and had been most disappointed when she had never worn it.

Tamara reached out a tentative hand and

stroked the smooth, rustling material thought-fully. Why not? It would please her aunt, and she was tired of the grays and browns that were the staple colors of her wardrobe. She certainly needed something to raise her morale if she were to get through the evening with her temper in-tact.

An hour later, her eyes widened slightly as she stared at her reflection in the full-length mirror. The gown was blazing crimson and almost me-dieval in cut, with long, tight sleeves and a fitted bodice, and the long skirt fell to the floor in graceful folds. The neckline was low and square-cut, showing a generous amount of cleavage, though it was probably quite modest compared to some of the gowns that would be on display tonight.

The gown took on its wicked provocation from Tamara herself. The combination of golden satin skin and a slim, curvaceous figure made all the difference.

The passionate curve of her lips, and the slightly slanted, wide-set violet eyes framed in extravagantly long lashes, lent her face a stormy sexuality that made her remember her aunt's simile of this afternoon. She'd said she looked like a king's mistress and that was certainly true tonight. She'd been trying to underplay that sultry, sexual quality for years, ever since that ghastly night at O'Malley's Roadhouse. Yet strangely, tonight she derived a certain amount of pleasure from seeing that brilliant bird of paradise in the mirror.

She quickly combed her long, silky black curls, then pulled her hair forward to nestle provocatively against the curve of her ripe breast. A glance at the clock on her bedside table verified that she still had forty-five minutes until Marc was due to arrive. She would go downstairs and wait.

She was halfway down the stairs when the doorbell buzzed stridently. Frowning in puzzlement, she continued slowly down the stairs, her eyes fixed on the shadowy outline behind the translucent panels of the front door. It couldn't be Marc. He firmly believed it was just as rude to be early as late, and would arrive at eight o'clock on the dot.

Besides, that masculine shadow had an odd electric quality that was totally unfamiliar to her. The shadow moved abruptly and suddenly the bell was ringing again. The visitor pushed on the bell with a rough impatience, causing Tamara's lips to tighten in displeasure as she hurried down the last few steps and across the hall. Whoever the visitor was, he could use a lesson in manners. She threw open the door.

"You certainly took your time about it, damn it!"

Tamara felt her mouth drop open in shock. The man standing before her was the most blatantly virile male she'd ever seen. He was in his late twenties or early thirties, a little under six feet, and every inch of his muscular body exuded an almost tangible sexual vitality. She'd sensed that electricity just from his shadowy silhouette, but it was nothing compared to the dynamic effect of his actual presence. Crisp dark hair, worn slightly long, framed features that were more fascinating than good-looking, she thought dazedly, except for that beautifully sensual mouth and the flashing dark eyes gazing at her with distinct displeasure.

The realization of this displeasure abruptly snapped her back to her usual cool sanity. Tamara wasn't used to that particular expression on the face of men who'd just seen her for the first time. She was more accustomed to their looks of dazed admiration than the open contempt of this arrogant and extremely rude man.

"May I help you?" she asked. Upon closer inspection, she was sure he'd come to the wrong house. She certainly had never seen him before, and it was unlikely her aunt was acquainted with a man like him. His biscuit-colored suit was obviously exorbitantly expensive and far too trendy for one of Aunt Elizabeth's conservative friends. His yellow linen shirt was left unbuttoned to reveal a strong bronze throat encircled by a fine gold chain.

"You must be the local vamp I've been hearing about," he said curtly, his dark eyes glittering. "Well, I'm sure you'd be very good at it, honey, but I've other fish to fry tonight. I want to speak to Elizabeth Ledford."

Tamara's eyes widened at the remark before a flush of anger stained her cheeks scarlet. This had to be the rudest, most conceited, most arrogant idiot she'd ever had the misfortune to meet. "My aunt is out for the evening," she said between clenched teeth. "Perhaps you could call her tomorrow for an appointment."

"No way!" he growled, a frown of impatience darkening his face. "I have to get back to New York tomorrow, and I intend to settle this tonight. I'll have to make do with you." He stepped aggressively into the hall, and Tamara was forced to move aside to avoid being swept out of his path. The nerve of the man!

"I'm afraid I also have plans for the evening so you'll have to leave *now*," she said crisply. She wasn't about to be intimidated by this macho lout!

His dark eyes narrowed dangerously. "I'd advise you to climb off that high horse. I'm mad as hell, and not in the mood for any of your histrionics, Cleopatra. You might find yourself occupying the same jail cell as your aunt if you're not careful."

"Jail! You're absolutely insane. Will you please get out of here?"

"When I do leave, it will be to go directly to the police. I don't think you'd want me to do that. I understand your great-aunt is a little old to be thrown into the holding tank, isn't she?" His voice was coolly ruthless, and Tamara felt a shiver of apprehension cutting through the antagonism she felt for this man.

"Who are you?" she asked.

"Rex Brody," he answered tautly. "And you're Tamara Ledford, right?"

"Right," she echoed. On reflection, all his remarks had betrayed an odd familiarity for a perfect stranger. "But how did you know that, Mr. Brody?"

His lips twisted cynically. "I know all about you, babe. I've spent the last two hours being filled in on all the juicy details of your aunt's operation. I even know about your little affair with Walter Bettencourt."

"My affair with—"

"I've got to admit I can understand his being unfaithful to my aunt a little better now that I've seen you," he drawled, his eyes lingering on the silken thrust of her breasts in the low-cut gown. "From what I hear, you have the reputation for being very accommodating to half the male population of this horse-and-buggy town. He'd have to be a monk to resist an experienced little madam like you."

"As I said before, you're completely crazy." Tamara's violet eyes were blazing. "I have no idea what you're talking about."

"Then perhaps we'd better discuss it," he suggested. "May I come in?"

He was already in, she thought in annoyance, as Brody shut the door and strode through the arched doorway to the right of the entry hall.

"Please do make yourself right at home, Mr. Brody," she said caustically, trailing behind him into the living room.

"Very cozy," he said, ignoring her sarcasm. "All this hominess must be very soothing to your 'clients,' Miss Ledford." There was a caustic barb in the smooth silkiness of his voice and Tamara clenched her fists in fury. Her gaze followed his around the room, noticing as if for the first time the faded flowered carpet, the worn spot on the shabby blue couch, and the lace drapes, yellowing with age, at the windows. Why did this arrogant, obnoxious man only have to enter the room for her suddenly to find fault with the only home she'd ever known?

The room *was* cozy, she thought defensively. What difference did it make that the furniture was old-fashioned and a bit shabby, and that lace doilies and family miniatures went out with high button shoes? It was all dear and familiar, and had the mellow graciousness of a faded but still beautiful old lady.

"This is our home, Mr. Brody," she said archly. "My aunt and I aren't concerned if the decor isn't up to your exalted standards." She sat down on the couch and gestured resignedly. "You might as well sit down."

He sat down on the couch beside her, looking bizarrely out of place in the gentle period surroundings. "You're very much on the defensive, Miss Ledford," he drawled. "I meant no offense. In fact, I think your aunt is much more clever than Celia Bettencourt imagines."

"Celia!" Tamara said sharply. "What does she have to do with this?"

"Did you actually think you could pull such an obvious scam on Aunt Margaret without her step-daughter tumbling to it?" he asked mockingly.

"Scam?" Tamara repeated, her violet eyes huge in her suddenly pale face. If Celia was involved in this crazy misunderstanding, then it foreboded serious trouble.

"Scam, bunko, con game. Whatever you care to call it, it's still highly illegal, Miss Ledford. I don't know how much your aunt has bilked Aunt Margaret out of in the last year on these phony psychic readings, but I want it returned double quick, do you understand?"

Tamara's chin lifted disdainfully. "I gather you're Margaret Bettencourt's nephew, Mr. Brody?" He nodded curtly, and she continued with acid sweetness. "How unfortunate for her. Do you always jump to conclusions without verifying the facts? For your information, my aunt never accepts money for her readings. When she's asked for help, she gives it without charge."

He nodded grimly. "I said she was clever, but not quite clever enough. She may not accept cash, but I think the police would agree that a pretty trinket would be valuable enough to constitute grand larceny." He gestured to a beautifully crafted Easter egg on the mantel. "I understand from Miss Bettencourt that my aunt gave Elizabeth Ledford this art object two months ago. Do you deny it?"

"Of course I don't deny it," Tamara said hotly. "Mrs. Bettencourt was very grateful to Aunt Elizabeth for her advice regarding some stock investments. She insisted on giving my aunt at least a token gift. It's quite lovely, but not at all valuable."

"Some token," he said, his lips twisting cynically. "Are you telling me you don't know that's a Fabergé egg, and it's worth a small fortune?"

"A Fabergé—" Tamara gasped, stunned. She shook her head dazedly. "You've got to be mistaken. Why would she give Aunt Elizabeth something so valuable?"

"Because my Aunt Margaret is basically a very naïve woman," Brody said grimly. "She must have been a piece of cake for your aunt to manipulate. There's no telling how much she's managed to get out of her in the past year." His dark eyes were staring thoughtfully at Tamara's shocked face. "Well, I'll be damned." He whistled. "You actually didn't know what your aunt was up to, did you?"

Tamara squared her shoulders proudly. "Of course I didn't realize the value of Mrs. Bettencourt's gift, and neither did my aunt. She would never have accepted it if she'd known it was anything but a trinket. I'm quite sure she'll return it immediately when I tell her."

"You're damn right she will," he said absently, still staring at her. There was an odd, flickering awareness in the depths of those dark eyes as his gaze moved from her face to her throat and then, in lingering assessment, to the full curve of her breasts. "Lord! You're a lovely creature!"

Tamara could feel the color rise to her face, and her breath caught in her throat. What in the world was wrong with her, she wondered with a panicky feeling in the pit of her stomach. All her cool assurance and control were gone in the time it had taken Rex Brody to give her that one burning glance. Why did the man have such an effect on her? She could feel her breasts tingle in response to that intimate appraisal, as though he were stroking her with his hand instead of his eyes.

She stood up abruptly and instinctively backed away from him. "Since we've agreed the egg will be returned to your aunt," she said a trifle breathlessly, "I believe that concludes our business, Mr. Brody."

"Do you?" Brody leaned back on the couch, his gaze running over her lazily; each inch of her flesh seemed to burn and come to vibrant life beneath the insolent caress of his eyes. "You're wrong, Tamara. I don't think we've even started."

He rose with liquid grace and crossed swiftly to where she stood. He was only inches away; she felt the heat emanating from his body and his shaving lotion reminded her vaguely of Russian Leather.

"I can't allow your aunt to continue her activities, you know," he said huskily. She could see by the quickening pulse in his throat he was as disturbed by her nearness as she was by his. "But that shouldn't affect your financial arrangements to any great degree. I'm sure we can work something out." His hand reached out almost compulsively to caress lightly the crimson taffeta covering her breasts and she could feel her nipples harden in response.

"What do you mean?" she asked throatily, her gaze fixed helplessly on his face. Was she going crazy? Why was she standing here allowing this stranger to caress her with an intimacy she'd never allowed any man?

"You know what I mean," Brody said thickly. His dark eyes were blazing now and he drew a deep, steadying breath. "I mean that you turn me on. We've got some wild chemistry working, pretty lady." He frowned impatiently. "Do you want it spelled out? I intend to take very good care of you. You needn't worry about that. I'm a great deal richer than Bettencourt." His lips tightened. "And I'm a helluva lot younger. I promise you that you won't regret coming to me, Tamara."

"Coming to you?" she repeated blankly. Then the color rushed to her face as she understood and was able at last to break the golden sensual threads that held her. The man was propositioning her as if she were a high-priced call girl! Well, why not, she thought bitterly. It was probably exactly what Celia had led him to believe she was. Understanding his reasons didn't modify her resentment toward him, however. Her violet eyes blazed. "Why should I come to you?" she asked recklessly. "Celia must have told you that I like variety in my lovers. Do you really think you could satisfy me?"

Brody's eyes blazed back at her. "I'm damn well sure I can," he said deliberately. "And so are you. You want it as much as I do." His hands reached out to grasp her shoulders. "And you'll just have to forget that penchant for variety. I'm going to be the only man in your bed from now on."

"The hell you will!" Tamara cried. She whirled away from him, her breasts heaving with fury. She glared back at him over her shoulder, her head lifted proudly. "I'm not going to occupy your bed or any portion of your life, Rex Brody! How do you have the nerve to come marching in here trying to intimidate Aunt Elizabeth, and then expect me to jump into bed with you!"

Her fury had no visible effect on Brody's cool demeanor. In fact, there was a glint of admiration mixed with amusement in his eyes. "I gather you're going to keep me in suspense for a while before you succumb to my fatal fascination," he said outrageously. "Well, I've never been known for my patience, but you just may be worth waiting for, Tamara Ledford."

"If you don't get out of here . . ." she stated threateningly, turning back to face him.

"Oh, I'm leaving," he said casually, strolling toward the door. He looked over his shoulder and winked mischievously. "I've got to get back to Bettencourt's to change for the party. I'll see you there, babe."

"Oh no you won't!" Tamara said. There was no way she was going to tolerate an evening of Rex Brody *and* Celia Bettencourt.

He paused at the door, all laughter banished from his face. "Yes, I will," he said, a steely determination firming his lips. "Don't even think about missing it, Tamara. I want you there tonight, and I make a habit of getting what I want. I've let the matter of your great-aunt's little criminal sideline slide for the moment, but don't think I've forgotten it. I assure you I'll remember it much more vividly and with considerably more activity if you're not at that party."

Before she could answer, Brody turned and walked out the door.

Two

THE BETTENCOURT MANSION was ablaze with lights as Marc Hellman turned his car into the long, curving driveway and drove carefully to the pillared front entrance. They were met by a white-jacketed servant, who smilingly helped Tamara from the dark blue Buick before taking Marc's car keys and tossing them to another servant so he could park the car.

Marc cupped Tamara's elbow protectively as they mounted the steps, and he bent his dark head to murmur quietly in her ear, "You're sure you want to go through with this? We could still send in a message with a servant. Walter surely wouldn't expect you to attend if he knew you were ill."

Tamara smiled reassuringly. "No, really, I'll be perfectly fine, Marc," she said. "It was just a headache. I'm much better now."

Marc Hellman shook his head, his thin, clever face concerned. "I'm not at all sure of that. You were shaking and practically in tears when I picked you up, and even now you're still quite flushed."

"Don't be silly, Marc, I'm perfectly well now," she said crossly, wishing he would stop fussing.

At times Marc's almost avuncular protectiveness could be quite annoying.

But a twinge of guilt pricked her at the worried frown on his face. He had arrived a scant five minutes after Brody had departed, and a plea of illness had been the first excuse she could think of to account for her obvious distress. Throughout dinner at Somerset's leading hotel, Marc had been extremely solicitous, even though she'd made every effort to appear normal.

She would dearly have loved to take Marc's suggestion that they miss the party, but she had a shrewd idea that the silken threat Brody had made before he'd left the house wasn't a bluff. For Aunt Elizabeth's sake she couldn't run the risk of his anger being directed at her, despite the indignation she felt. She'd just have to make another attempt to convince him Aunt Elizabeth had never had any intention of accepting compensation for her services, and that this whole misunderstanding was utterly ridiculous.

She preceded Marc quickly through the front door, leaving her cloak with the servant in attendance in the front entrance hall, and moved swiftly to the left where Walter, Margaret, and Celia Bettencourt formed a receiving line to greet their guests.

Walter smiled with genuine pleasure as he took her hand in his. "Tamara, how good it is to have you here, my dear. You're looking positively radiant tonight. You should wear red more often."

"Thank you, Mr. Bettencourt," Tamara replied warmly. "You're looking very dashing yourself." She spoke only the truth. Walter Bettencourt was in his early fifties, but his vigorous, athletic body was fit and lean and his features had a blunt cragginess that was very attractive. "And Mrs. Bettencourt looks absolutely ravishing," she added.

Occupied for the moment with greeting another guest, Margaret Bettencourt didn't hear the compliment, but her husband beamed proudly at his attractive brunette wife in her peach silk gown. "She certainly does. How do you suppose a staid old businessman like me got so lucky?"

Just then Margaret Bettencourt looked up and smiled with a warm kindness that lit her charming face. "I'm so glad you've come, Tamara," she said. There was a flush of color on her cheeks and her gentle gray eyes were glowing with excitement. "There's someone I want you to meet."

Walter Bettencourt slipped an arm about his wife's slim waist and said with an indulgent chuckle, "That's what she's been saying to everyone. Personally, I think this nephew of yours is just a myth. You've been telling me about the man since the day I met you and I've yet even to see this paragon."

His wife cast him an affectionately reproving

glance. "I explained that Rex has been in London for the past sixteen months. You would have met him early this evening if he hadn't suddenly been called away on business."

Some business, Tamara thought grimly. Attempting to harass a helpless old woman! "I don't believe I've ever heard you speak of a nephew, Mrs. Bettencourt," she murmured.

Margaret Bettencourt made a wry face. "I guess it's become a way of life over the years to keep a low profile where Rex is concerned. The poor boy has so little privacy I've always been a bit overprotective, I'm afraid."

"That's an understatement if I ever heard one," Walter Bettencourt said, his eyes twinkling. "You didn't even tell Celia that we have a celebrity in the family until today."

"Celebrity?" Tamara frowned in puzzlement. Margaret Bettencourt began to explain when Celia's dulcet voice chimed into the conversation.

"Tamara, darling, how utterly fabulous you look. What an *interesting* gown." Celia's smile was saccharine sweet.

For interesting read bizarre, Tamara thought dryly, as the pencil slim blonde scanned the crimson gown with barely concealed envy in her limpid brown eyes. Celia herself was gowned with svelte sophistication in a black strapless dress that hugged her slender figure with frank boldness. Her ash blond hair was piled high in a fashionable crown of curls on top of her head, and her elaborately applied makeup gave her delicate features a doll-like prettiness.

"Thank you, Celia," Tamara replied quietly. "How very kind of you."

"I was just telling Tamara she should wear bright colors more often, Celia," her father said heartily. "Doesn't she look stunning?"

"Yes, quite stunning," Celia echoed hollowly. She turned abruptly to Marc Hellman, who'd been quietly complimenting his hostess, and smiled brilliantly. "How are you, Marc?"

At least Celia was behaving with a surface civility, Tamara noted with relief. Perhaps she'd expended all her troublemaking potential for one day with that last imbroglio she'd provoked by her malicious tale-bearing to Brody.

It was another few seconds before they could break away and Tamara breathed a sigh of relief when Marc, a hand beneath her elbow, gently propelled her across the crowded ballroom to a quiet corner. He deftly commandeered two drinks from a passing waiter.

"Quite a crowd," he commented casually, as he looked around the large room appraisingly. "I don't believe Walter has thrown a party of this size since Natalie died."

"You knew his first wife?" Tamara asked, surprised. Then she bit her lower lip vexedly as Marc's face tightened in annoyance. Of course he would have known Natalie Bettencourt. Her employer couldn't be more than five years older than Marc. She was continually forgetting how much older Marc was than she, but she was aware how sensitive he was on the subject. He certainly didn't look anywhere near the forty-seven he was. His dark hair was only lightly frosted with gray at the temples and an almost fanatic devotion to tennis kept his tall, slim figure firm and muscular.

"Yes, I went to school with Natalie," Marc admitted stiffly.

"Tamara, you look absolutely fantastic!"

Tamara turned with scarcely disguised relief at Janie Sutherland's exclamation. Her young sales assistant was looking very attractive herself in a spring green gown that set off her glossy brown hair to perfection. She didn't wait for Tamara's response before rushing on eagerly. "I suppose Celia couldn't wait to tell you about the social lion she's acquired in the family. She's going to be absolutely ghastly to be around now that she has a superstar like Rex Brody to flaunt. Not that she was any prize before."

"Superstar?" Tamara asked, puzzled again. "Rex Brody?"

Janie's eyes widened in incredulous surprise. "You're not telling me you've never heard of him?" she asked. "Good heavens, the man is world famous! I know you're a classical music fan, but you must have heard about Rex Brody. He was the hottest singer in America before he quit performing four years ago to concentrate on composing. Since then he's won a Tony for the best Broadway musical and an Oscar for the best original song for a motion picture. You must have seen him last year on television when he accepted the Academy Award."

"We don't have a television set. Aunt Elizabeth won't have one in the house," Tamara said absently. So that was why Brody had that air of arrogant self-assurance. If he was as famous as Janie indicated, it was no wonder he felt he could just walk in and take whatever he wanted.

"I've heard Brody's score for *Lost Dream*," Marc said thoughtfully. "It's an exceptional piece of work."

Tamara looked at him in disbelief. Marc hated pop music with a passion. In fact, it was their mutual love of the classics that had brought him and Tamara together.

"That's not the only exceptional piece of work," Janie drawled, winking. "The man practically oozes sex appeal. When he announced he was returning to performing and going on tour, his concerts were sold out all over the country six hours after the tickets went on sale. He's supposed to appear in New York day after tomorrow and I've read that the scalpers are already asking two hundred dollars a ticket."

"Very impressive," Tamara said with a coolness she was far from feeling. Every word Janie was uttering was increasing the feelings of trepidation and anxiety that had beset her since Brody had left her earlier. Aunt Elizabeth's situation was far worse than she'd imagined: Brody had power and prestige.

"I'm surprised Celia didn't tell you about him," Janie said, obviously curious. "She's certainly been boasting about him to all and sundry. Everyone in the room is waiting with bated breath for the great man to arrive."

"It's not very courteous of him to be late for his aunt's anniversary party," Marc said with a disapproving frown.

"According to Celia, he had some very important business to take care of and only arrived back at ye old family mansion a short while ago," Janie said, her eyes twinkling mischievously. "If he hadn't just arrived in town today, I'd be tempted to wonder if there was a woman involved."

Tamara could feel the heat rush to her cheeks at Janie's accidental verbal score. She could imagine the gossip that would have ensued if anyone had observed that scene in Aunt Elizabeth's living room.

"Are you sure you're feeling well, my dear?" Marc asked worriedly. "You're really quite flushed."

"I feel absolutely wonderful," she lied. "It's just a trifle warm in here." She took a quick and overlarge swallow of her drink and gave him a dazzling smile.

Rex Brody didn't make his appearance for another forty-five minutes, and in that time Tamara had consumed two more martinis. Unaccustomed as she was to liquor, she found the drinks had the beneficial effect of loosening the cold knot of tension in her breast and replacing it with a bittersweet recklessness.

She was dancing with Marc when she heard a stir and then a low rustle of whispering that ran through the room like wind through a wheat field. She didn't even have to look toward the door to realize what had caused the stir. When she did glance over Marc's shoulder, she could only glimpse Brody's raven head because of the crush of people that had surged forward to surround him.

She was conscious of a feeling of relief when she realized she wouldn't have to confront him immediately. From the look of the crowd around him, it would be impossible for him to break free for some time.

"Pardon me, Marc, may I cut in?" The voice was deep and mocking, and Tamara jerked her head up in surprise.

"Hello, Todd," she said coolly, as Marc politely relinquished her and left the dance floor. She was glad now she'd had those martinis. Todd Jamison, Celia Bettencourt's fiancé, was looking down at her with an openly hungry look that was mixed with active dislike. As they began to dance, Tamara noted how attractive Todd's tall, athletic form was in evening clothes. His carefully styled blond hair and classical features, together with that intriguing cleft in his chin, had always been devastatingly appealing to women. It was no wonder he was spoiled. His good looks and his father's money had always gotten Todd exactly what he wanted.

No, not always. He hadn't gotten what he wanted that night at O'Malley's Roadhouse, and his malice had marred Tamara's relationships in all the years since.

"Lord, you're gorgeous tonight," he breathed hoarsely, as they moved slowly around the floor. "You're like a flame burning out of control in that gown."

"I assure you I'm quite in control, Todd," she said icily, looking up at him. "Which is the only reason I'm dancing with you now. You knew I wouldn't want to cause a scene in the middle of the dance floor."

"You always were a bright girl, Tamara," he said, his lips tightening. "I knew you wouldn't be too crazy about dancing with me, but I didn't give a damn." His arms tightened around her as he dragged her closer.

"You've got to be either drunk or crazy, Todd Jamison," she hissed, straining to get away from him. "Let me go! I've had enough problems with that charming fiancée of yours today without your adding to them. Go dance with Celia, for heaven's sake!"

"I've had a few drinks," he admitted, burying his face in her hair. "You always smell like gardenias," he said thickly.

He'd had more than a few drinks, Tamara thought grimly. As monumentally self-centered as Todd was, he was usually more discreet in his advances. She should know; she'd been fending them off for years.

"Why don't you give up, Todd?" she said, trying to keep her voice even. "You know I can't stand you. I despise you more than anyone I've ever known. Why can't you just leave me alone?"

"Do you think I don't want to?" he asked bitterly. "Sometimes I think I really hate you, but it doesn't seem to matter. I've wanted you so long that it's become like a sickness. Half the time I want to strangle you, and the other half I want to drag you off to bed."

"That's hardly new, is it, Todd?" she asked caustically. "Since when have you ever wanted to do anything else? You always did reach out to grab what you wanted, and you never gave a damn who you hurt. I learned that lesson a long time ago."

An angry flush stained Jamison's face and he frowned sulkily. "How many times do I have to apologize for that night? So I got a little carried away and got a little rough. I told you I've always been crazy about you. What could you expect when you led me on and then turned me down at the last minute?"

Despite her resolve to retain her composure, Tamara could feel a swift surge of rage electrify her. "I was sixteen years old and green as grass. I hadn't a clue about what it even meant to 'lead a boy on,'" she flared, her violet eyes flashing fire. "And if you call attempted rape 'a little rough,' I'm afraid I can't agree with the euphemism."

"Everyone at school knew what went on at O'Malley's," Jamison said belligerently. "Yet you agreed to go there that night without even an argument. Naturally I expected you to put out."

"I didn't know what kind of place it was, and you knew very well I didn't." Her lips curved in a bitter smile. "All I knew was that the wonderful, popular football hero, Todd Jamison, had asked me for a date." She shook her head wonderingly, her eyes sad as she looked back on that naïve, starry-eyed teenager. "Green as grass."

There was a flare of hope in Todd's eyes. "You admit you had a yen for me once," he said eagerly. "I can teach you to feel like that again. Let me take you home tonight, Tamara."

Her eyes widened. "Do you really think I could forget everything you did to me?" she asked. "There's a remote possibility I may be able to forgive you for attacking me, but not for what you did afterward. Do you know what misery you caused me with all those lies? You nearly destroyed me, damn it!"

"You hurt my pride," he defended, with the arrogant egotism of a spoiled child. "All the guys were hot for you, and when I told them you were going with me to O'Malley's, they were jealous as hell. I couldn't tell them you'd run out on me. They'd have laughed at me."

"So instead you made me out to be the hottest lay in town and certainly the most promiscuous," she said scornfully. "You must have been very convincing, Todd. I couldn't even go to the malt shop with a boy without him trying to drag me to the nearest motel. It became the thing for every boy I dated to claim he'd slept with me."

"And did they?" Jamison asked hoarsely, his arms tightening around her. "It used to drive me crazy listening to them bragging about all the things they'd done with you, and not knowing whether they'd really scored when I couldn't."

"You've got to be the most contemptible low-life on the face of the earth," Tamara said. "Doesn't it even matter to you that you're engaged to Celia?"

He shook his head. "I told you that you were almost an obsession with me," he said huskily. "If you crooked your little finger, I'd drop her in a minute and come running. Do you know that I dream about you at night?"

"I can imagine what kind of dreams," she said disgustedly. "Well, don't be in any hurry to sacrifice that Jamison-Bettencourt merger, Todd. It will be a cold day in July when I encourage you to do anything but leave me alone."

There was a touch of cockiness in Jamison's smile as he drawled insolently, "If I'm patient enough, I'll get what I want. You won't hold out forever, Tamara. Anyone can tell by just looking at you what a hot number you are. Do you think anyone's been fooled by that demure air you put on? They still remember those stories you're so eager to live down. You should hear them talk about you in the locker room at the country club. Every man in town knows you're just playing it cool until you nab Marc Hellman." He pulled her still closer. "You'll get tired of Hellman. And when you do, I'll be there waiting."

Before she could reply to this outrageous statement, the music ended. She broke away from Todd's hold and stalked away feeling as if she were aflame with rage.

"Tamara?"

She whirled to face Marc Hellman, her face stormy, her violet eyes shooting sparks. Gazing challengingly into his thin face, she asked tersely, "Marc, what do you see when you look at me?"

He stared at her blankly. "I beg your pardon?"

He frowned worriedly. "Tamara, I think I'd better take you home. You've been quite unlike yourself this evening."

She laughed recklessly. "Really? Perhaps I should rephrase the question. What kind of person do you think I am, Marc?"

"Why . . ." He gestured helplessly. "You're intelligent, dignified, and gentle. You have a quiet charm and are very discriminating." He shook his head. "Why are you behaving this way, my dear?"

She stared at him in sad amazement. She had thought that Marc knew her better than anyone in Somerset, yet the person he had described was no closer to her own personality than Todd's assessment. Did everyone see only what they wanted to see? She suddenly felt terribly alone.

"Perhaps because the woman you've just described has all the characteristics of a victim," she replied huskily. "And I find I'm tired of acting a part to try to gain approval from people who couldn't care less about who I really am. I've been trying to conform to Somerset's idea of what a lady should be since I was sixteen. I've been as discreet and colorless as a little brown wren for years, but I'm still looked upon as some kind of scarlet woman."

"You're speaking wildly, Tamara," Marc said in a firm, fatherly voice.

She shook her head, turned, and disappeared into the crowd.

The emotional shocks that had followed one upon the other had shattered the cocoon Tamara had woven around her feelings, and she was flooded with a wild euphoria that made her peculiarly light-headed. Not that the three cocktails she'd consumed earlier hadn't contributed to that state, she thought ruefully. Whatever the cause, it resulted in the banishing of her inhibitions and she found the new Tamara Ledford to be bitterly amusing.

If no amount of discretion was going to change anyone's opinion of her, why should she attempt the impossible? Why not enjoy herself and give everyone what they expected of her? Since they thought of her as some sort of *femme fatale*, then she'd show them just how vampish she could be if she put her mind to it.

She found it ridiculously easy. All it took was a slow, seductive smile or an alluring sidelong glance and her partners responded as if she'd pushed the ignition button on a rocket. She soon had a small court of eager males around her, vying for her favors. She was aware of the whispers and coldly disapproving glances she was receiving from the other women in the room, but that didn't really matter until she looked up to meet the eyes of Celia Bettencourt.

The blonde was standing only a few yards away. She was holding Todd Jamison's arm with possessive intimacy, but her attention was fixed with malevolence on Tamara and her circle of admirers. Her voice was light but meant to carry clearly to the people in her immediate vicinity. "Isn't it amusing to see the little bastard try her hand at social climbing? But then who could blame her after living all her life with that crazy old witch of an aunt?"

At the blatant insult, rage shot through Tamara like a lightning bolt. She'd taken just about enough from Celia for one day. There was a look of embarrassed shock on the faces of most of the crowd surrounding them. The rudeness had been too obvious for even Celia's most devoted syco- phants to accept. It was clear Tamara was meant to be hurt and humiliated by the comment, and that only served to increase the tide of anger flowing through her. She might have tried to ig- nore an insult to herself, but there was no way she was going to take Celia's sniping at Aunt Elizabeth without retaliation.

Her eyes narrowed as her gaze moved thought- fully to Todd Jamison. Judging by the flush on his face and the slight sway of his body as he returned her look hungrily, he'd clearly been im- bibing heavily since she'd seen him last. For a moment she hesitated. What she was about to do went much against the grain, and she almost surrendered the idea at its birth. Then Celia fol- lowed her remark with a burst of scornful laugh- ter.

What had Todd said earlier? Oh yes, that he would come to her if she so much as crooked her little finger. Well, he was about to be put to the test, she thought grimly.

She smiled, putting every bit of voltage and appeal she possessed into it. Then, raising her hand, she languidly beckoned Jamison to come to her. At first she thought he was ignoring the gesture. He didn't move and there was a dazed, blank expression on his face. Then he brushed Celia's hand from his arm as if she didn't exist and started eagerly forward.

"Todd!" Celia's exclamation was charged with incredulity and outrage, but he acted as if he hadn't heard her. He was so soused he probably hadn't, Tamara thought wryly.

Then suddenly there was a sound from Celia that was a cross between a snarl and a shriek as she rushed forward, pushing Todd Jamison out of her way, to halt before Tamara. She was breathing hard, her doll-like face suddenly not pretty at all, her eyes glazed with fury.

"Damn you!" she hissed, and her hand swung out to connect with a sharp crack on Tamara's cheek.

For an instant Tamara couldn't believe it had happened. Even Celia wouldn't cause such a scene at her father's anniversary celebration! But she'd done it, as was evidenced by the sudden, shocked silence of the guests.

"If you'll excuse me, please," Tamara said formally. She raised her chin proudly and with a slow, regal dignity glided through the silent crowd to the French doors that led to the terrace.

THREE

As TAMARA CLOSED the doors, she heard the sudden outbreak of conversation behind her. She leaned back for a moment, the cool breeze stroking her hot cheeks like a caressing hand. The reckless gaiety and daring that had sustained her through the evening had abruptly subsided, drowned in the shock and embarrassment she'd felt in that terrible moment when Celia Bettencourt had attacked her.

She felt only a deep depression now as she straightened slowly and wandered despondently to the decorative stone wall bordering the flagstone terrace. She gazed blindly out over the formal rose garden as silent tears ran slowly down her cheeks.

"Well, you're certainly well versed in the art of raising hell, sweetheart," Rex Brody drawled behind her.

Tamara whirled to face him, her stance as defensive as an animal at bay.

Brody leisurely closed the French doors behind him and moved toward her with lithe grace. The moonlight flooding the patio illuminated his tuxedo-clad figure in dramatic, black-and-white relief, and if anything he appeared more magnetic than ever in the formal attire.

She didn't answer, afraid he would detect her momentary weakness in the shakiness of her voice. She turned hurriedly away again, not daring to wipe her eyes. The blasted moonlight was almost as bright as the noon sun and she'd be damned if she'd reveal to Brody how vulnerable she felt at this moment. He was already dealing from a position of power without her weeping before him like a woeful child.

He halted next to her, gazing down at the dark silkiness of her averted head. "You ought to be spanked, you know," he said grimly. "After you move in with me, I'll break your little neck if you pull anything like this again."

"*I* deserve to be punished!" she exploded indignantly, only hearing those first outrageous words. "I'm the one who was slapped by your dear cousin-in-law in front of an entire room of people. I'm the one who was insulted. Don't you think she should reap a bit of the blame?"

"What did you expect after the way you behaved all evening? You threw out so many lures you had every man in the room reeling. You're fortunate one of those women whose man you filched didn't take a knife to you. I'd say you got off damn lucky."

"How do you know how I've been behaving all evening? I haven't even seen you since you walked in the door. You've been so surrounded by all your fans I'm sure you haven't had time to do anything but absorb all their adoring gush."

"You may not have seen me, but I assure you I've kept an eagle eye on you," Brody said mockingly. "You've been very visible indeed, love. At first I was merely amused by your antics. I must admit you play Circe with more panache than I've ever seen it done, and as a performer myself, I have a certain admiration for style." His mouth tightened. "I was about to put a stop to your little charade when you decided to put the crowning touch on your achievement by bewitching little Cousin Celia's property. That was a bad move, darling."

"I thought I did it very well," Tamara said, a thread of bitterness running through her voice. "Though in Todd's case it was really no challenge. Circe wouldn't have wasted her time on Todd. He's already a swine."

Brody gave a soundless whistle. "I believe I detect a note of passion in that lovely voice," he said thoughtfully. "I think perhaps I'll have a little talk with Todd Jamison."

"Passion! I hate the man," she cried, and suddenly those maddening tears began to fall again.

"I don't care what you feel for him," Brody said with soft menace. "It's enough that you feel something. I find I'm becoming quite possessive of you, Tamara Ledford."

Tamara shook her head dazedly. "You're not

making any sense. I don't know what you're talking about, and at the moment I don't care," she said huskily. "Will you please just leave me alone?"

Brody swore under his breath at the sudden break in her voice. He reached out swiftly and grasped her by the shoulders and turned her to face him, tilting her head back with one hand so he could look into her face.

"Oh hell's bells, you're crying!" he said incredulously. His dark eyes probed her face mercilessly, noting every nuance of pain and unhappiness in the shaking of her lips, the swift veiling of her eyes as she closed her lids. "Damn it all, you let them hurt you in there. I thought you were one tough lady, but you're just a kid," he said wonderingly.

"No, you're wrong," she said, trying to turn her face away from that scalpel-keen appraisal. "I'll be all right in a moment. It was just the shock."

"Shut up, sweetheart," Brody said, and swept her into his arms, holding her as warmly and securely as if she were a baby. His hands moved gently up and down her back in a magically soothing caress. "Just be quiet and let me hold you. I promise you nothing will ever hurt you again while I'm around."

She believed him. It seemed impossible this was the same man whose nearness had turned her into liquid fire only a few hours before. It was as if he'd switched off that virile magnetism and electric vitality and was offering her only the warmth and tenderness she so desperately needed at the moment. She buried her head in his shoulder and let the tears flow freely while he rocked her in his arms, murmuring inaudible words of comfort and reassurance. His hands caressed and massaged her back and he dropped an occasional butterfly kiss on her temple or the curve of her neck. It was all so deliciously healing and secure Tamara felt she could stay there forever, being stroked and cosseted by this complex man who'd turned her life upside down in only a few hours. She didn't know when her arms went around his waist to hold him closer or when the tears stopped and were replaced by a dreamy contentment.

"You know that this changes things, of course," Brody whispered huskily, as he reached up to tangle a hand in her silky black hair. He tilted her head back to look into her face, catching his breath at the expression of glowing contentment and languid radiance illuminating it. "Don't you know weeping is supposed to make a lady's face swollen and ugly?" He touched her wet, dark lashes with a gentle finger. "It's not supposed to make your eyes look like violets after rain. Didn't anyone ever tell you that?"

"I guess not," Tamara whispered, looking up at his face so close to her own. She hadn't noticed before how long and thick Brody's black lashes were, she thought languidly, or how truly beautiful the cut of that sensual mouth.

"Well, they should have," he said huskily. "It's totally unfair you should look like this right now. It's the unexpected that lays a man low every time." He shook his head as if to clear it and then moved backward, unwinding her arms from around his waist and putting her firmly from him. "We've got to talk, and I find I'm just as susceptible as your other little conquests tonight. So keep your distance. Okay?"

Tamara felt a shaky chilliness and desolation now that she was no longer in the warm circle of his arms, and it served to rip away the languid contentment he'd so easily woven around her. She was jarred abruptly back to her senses. What on earth had she been thinking of?

"Yes, of course," she said confusedly, backing hurriedly away from him. "I'm afraid I lost control for a moment. I apologize for weeping all over you. It must have been very embarrassing."

"Hush, sweetheart," Brody said, his dark eyes twinkling. "I enjoyed every moment of it, and you'd still be in my arms if I thought I could think straight with you cuddling up to me like a little girl with her favorite teddy bear. Unfortunately I'm finding my paternal attitude is fading fast, and I don't think you'd want the type of comfort I'm prepared to give at the moment." He leaned back against the balustrade and gazed at her ruefully. "I thought I had it all worked out, but I'm afraid you've blasted all my plans to shrapnel."

"I don't know what you're talking about." Tamara shook her head. "I didn't do anything."

"Oh yes you did, lovely lady," he said mockingly. "You wept. I find I can't stand to see you cry, it tears me apart." His lips twisted wryly. "I remember once when I was a boy, I saw a 'Star Trek' episode on TV about an incredibly lovely alien who could completely bewitch any man by merely letting fall a tear or two. I thought it was the most arrant piece of nonsense imaginable. Now I'm not at all sure."

"Oh no, not again!" Tamara cried indignantly. This was just too much! Placing her hands on her hips, she glared belligerently at him. "Today you've called me everything from Cleopatra to Circe and now you're comparing me to some futuristic *femme fatale*!" She punched a finger at his broad chest and said hotly, "Well, I've had enough! For your information, Mr. Brody, I'm an intelligent, modern businesswoman and I haven't the faintest desire to tempt you strong macho men to do anything but jump into the Atlantic Ocean!"

She saw to her extreme exasperation that there

was an indulgent grin on Brody's face and a decided twinkle in the midnight dark eyes. "You can scarcely blame us for romanticizing you," he said, one eyebrow arching whimsically. "We poor males have a rough time finding a woman who can transport us back to the days when knighthood was in flower. But I've changed my mind about your being Circe. You're more like Helen of Troy or Guinevere."

"That's hardly much better," Tamara said with a grimace. "They were both unfaithful wives, as I recall."

"But with a subtle difference. They were as much victims of their own allure as the men they enchanted," Brody said lightly. "That's why wars were fought over them. Who can resist a tragic maiden in distress? Even I feel an urge to go out and fight a dragon or two when you look up at me with those big pansy eyes."

"I can fight my own dragons, thank you," she said crossly. "The only thing I need is for you to drop this ridiculous persecution of Aunt Elizabeth and go back to cavorting at your rock concerts."

"Cavorting!" he exclaimed. "Is that what you think of my performance?" He drew himself up majestically. "I do *not* cavort."

Her lips twitched in reluctant amusement. It seemed she'd scored a hit on a very sensitive nerve. "I meant no offense, Mr. Brody. I've never seen you perform," she said, gazing demurely at him from beneath her lashes. "I thought all rock stars cavorted."

"What a damnably condescending description! And for your information, I'm not a rock star."

"Whatever," Tamara said with a shrug, and this seemed to please him even less.

"You've really never seen me perform?" he asked, shaking his dark head disbelievingly. With the simple endearing egotism of a child, he added, "I didn't think that was possible."

She smothered an involuntary smile and tried to frown sternly at him. "This is all completely nonessential, Mr. Brody," she said briskly. "Now, will you permit Aunt Elizabeth to return that gift and forget about all this nonsense of pressing charges?"

"Oh yes, your Aunt Elizabeth," he said absently, and Tamara had the odd impression he'd forgotten about the threat that had made her almost frantic with worry. Then his dark eyes became shuttered and he once more leaned back against the balustrade and smiled mockingly. "It's not going to be that easy, sweetheart. I happen to be as protective of my aunt as you seem to be of yours. I'm afraid I'm going to need a hostage for your aunt's future good behavior."

"A hostage?" Tamara asked warily. "You can't mean you're still suggesting that I become your mistress?"

"Oh yes, I still intend that you occupy my bed eventually," he said gently, his dark eyes regretful. "But I must admit you've complicated things enormously by appealing to my protective instincts. When I thought you were just a tough little cookie with a fantastic body, I was sure we could negotiate a mutually pleasant exchange of favors." He sighed morosely. "Now I guess I'll have to resort to a little blackmail."

"Blackmail can be a very ugly crime, Mr. Brody," she said, her voice shaking with anger.

"Just calm down, sweetheart," he said coolly. "I've no intention of inviting you into my bed until you're as eager to go there as I am. I like my women willing. All I'm bargaining for at the moment is the pleasure of your company for the next four weeks. I open in New York day after tomorrow, and then I go on a cross-country tour. I want you to come with me."

"Come with you?" Tamara repeated, feeling as if she were caught in the center of a whirlwind. "You mean you want me to just drop everything, disrupt my entire life, and trail around with you like some sort of camp follower?"

"Yep," he drawled blandly. "That about covers it. In return, I promise to leave your slightly larcenous relative to her own devices as long as they don't involve Aunt Margaret. I'll also promise not to bed you until you say the word."

"You have it all worked out," she observed dryly. "Didn't it occur to you that I do have a career of my own? I just can't abandon it to become your own private groupie."

"I hardly think Bettencourt will be too enthusiastic about retaining your services after the debacle this evening," Brody said, a glint of sympathy in his eyes. "No matter how valuable an employee you are or how close you were in the past, I got the distinct impression tonight that he's very fond of his Celia. If it comes down to choices, you'll be out on your ear, love."

She wondered uneasily if he were right. Despite Walter Bettencourt's business acumen, he'd always been blindly indulgent in matters concerning his daughter. Was all the work and effort of the past five years to be wiped out in a matter of hours?

Brody frowned with concern when he saw the stricken look on Tamara's face, and he moved instinctively to cradle her once again in his arms. "Hey, don't," he said huskily, as he buried his face in her hair. "You look like a little girl who's just lost her favorite doll. I told you I can't stand that." He rocked her tenderly, while his deep voice murmured consolingly. "Who in the hell cares about Bettencourt's job anyway? At the end of the tour, I'll buy you your own flower shop anywhere you want to set up. How about Rodeo Drive?"

"Herb shop," she corrected automatically, and then chuckled. "I think you actually mean it. One minute you're blackmailing me and the next you're giving me the most fabulous present imaginable. Are you always this generous?"

"It's only money," he said and shrugged. "I've pots of the stuff. Why shouldn't I replace your doll, little girl?" His deep voice was like dark honey.

Tamara felt her throat tighten helplessly. This particular Rex Brody was much more dangerous than the sexy aggressor who had brought her body to electric awareness early this evening. It was so hard to fight his warm, touching, caring, and almost boyish sincerity. Nevertheless, she said huskily, "I'm a big girl and I buy my own toys now. I couldn't accept your offer, Mr. Brody."

His arms tightened about her. "We'll work something out. I'll advance you the money as a long-term loan."

She shook her head, trying hard not to smile. "You're certainly offering extravagantly generous terms for your bargain. You know you've no real guarantee of getting what you want, don't you?"

He tilted her head back and his hand stroked the curve of her cheek with sensuous enjoyment. "You have the most exquisite skin. It's like warm satin," he said. She stood quite docilely, still curiously content under that caressing touch, almost as if he had a perfect right to stroke and caress her. This remarkable man had the most extraordinary effect on her, Tamara thought in bewilderment. She would move out of his arms in a moment, she promised herself. But there was no threat in that gentle touch, and it was pleasurable to let herself be fondled like a beloved child.

"I fully expect to get what I want, love," he said lazily. "We're a highly combustible mixture, and I assure you I'm going to bend all my efforts toward a Fourth-of-July explosion. Besides, there are any number of women who are attracted to the glamour of the spotlight and make a nuisance of themselves. A beauty like you would prove a valuable deterrent."

"And what if I resist your fatal charm and

refuse to occupy your bed for the entire month?" she asked curiously.

"Then you walk away with your aunt free and clear, and an exclusive little boutique on Rodeo Drive. You also have the satisfaction of seeing me with egg on my face," he said lightly.

Her eyes narrowed. "I think I may call your bluff. I don't think you'll really press charges against my Aunt Elizabeth if I don't go with you."

His hand stopped its stroking and dropped to her shoulders. "Don't try it, babe," he warned so softly that Tamara barely detected the steely menace in his voice until she noticed the faint hardening of his lips and the dangerous flicker in the dark eyes. "I grew up as a slum kid on the streets of New York and I never learned how to bluff. If you couldn't deliver what you promised, then you ended up in a gutter or a hospital bed. Don't make the mistake of thinking I don't mean exactly what I say."

She twisted away from him with a little nervous shiver. How could she have forgotten her first impression of Brody? He was every bit the tough, menacing stranger of that first meeting. He was all the more dangerous for the chameleon quality that allowed him to alter his personality at will and keep his antagonists in a constant state of imbalance.

"Oh, I believe you, Mr. Brody," she said. "I'm quite sure you can be just as unscrupulous as you say. I suppose I'll have to agree to your terms, but at the end of that month, I want nothing from you but my release." Her mouth tightened. "You're going to look funny with egg on your face."

He smiled gently, his eyes once more warm and caressing. "We'll have to see about that, won't we, love?" He leaned forward and gave her a quick, impudent kiss on the tip of her nose. "Now I think I'd better take you home. You've had enough strain to cope with this evening. Shall I get your wrap and bring it to you here?"

She nodded wearily, feeling suddenly as exhausted as if she'd fought a major battle. And so she had, she thought ruefully, and a losing one at that. "Yes, please. It's a black velvet cloak."

He nodded and started off, only to turn back

abruptly. "We don't have to leave right now, you know," he said, his gaze searching. "You had a pretty rough time in there this evening. If you'd like to go in and get some of your own back, I usually have enough clout to carry the day. Being a celebrity has its uses."

Her mouth dropped open in amazement. "You'd do that for me?"

He shrugged. "Why not? I'd probably enjoy it."

"Well, I wouldn't," she said with a moue of distaste. "But I'm surprised you'd be willing to antagonize your aunt's guests just so I could enjoy a form of very petty revenge."

"When you agreed to my terms, you became both my property and my responsibility for the next month," he explained simply. "You'll find I know how to protect my own. I'll get your cloak, and I'll call off that date of yours."

He was gone before she could reply, and she stared after him in amazement. The terrace seemed suddenly terribly empty and lifeless now that his vital presence was gone, and she felt oddly weak and defenseless. Which was utterly absurd, she assured herself firmly. It must be weariness and discouragement that were making her so foolish.

Brody was back in the space of a few minutes and he took charge again with the almost royal confidence she was becoming accustomed to. Draping the black velvet cloak around her, he buttoned it carefully while she stared at him bemusedly, feeling like a small child being readied for Sunday School.

A little of that fugitive amusement must have been reflected on her face, for when he'd finished he looked up with a mischievous grin. "Sorry to be so slow, sweetheart. I promise you I'm much more dexterous at getting a lady *out* of her clothes."

She just bet he was. Even when dampened down that virile magnetism was almost overpoweringly potent, and combined with the wealth and glamour surrounding his profession, he would be practically irresistible to women. For some reason this thought irritated her exceedingly, and she maintained a remote silence while he whisked her along the flagstone path around to the front of the house.

A silver Ferrari was waiting at the front entrance. A servant jumped out of the driver's seat and handed Brody the car keys, then with flattering obsequiousness helped Tamara into the passenger seat. The wine plush velvet upholstery of the sports car was as luxurious as the car's exterior, and she sank into the cushioned softness with a sigh of relief. This macabre evening was almost at an end and she could feel fatigue wrap her in a numb lassitude.

Brody shot a concerned glance at the mauve shadows beneath her violet eyes, which gave her face a haunting fragility. "Try to relax," Brody ordered as he put the car in gear and started down the circular driveway. "As I recall, it's about a thirty-minute drive." He patted the steering wheel affectionately. "And Ole Dobbin knows the way home."

She had to smile at the absurdity of comparing this sleek, futuristic monster with a farm horse, and she leaned her head back obediently on the headrest. The motion of the car was smooth and effortless, and the powerful motor purred with the hypnotic growl of a jungle cat. It was rather like its owner in that respect, Tamara thought. Sleek, compact, graceful, and very, very danger. . . .

Aunt Elizabeth had definitely put too much starch in the pillowcases and they had a strange musky odor, most unlike their usual fresh, outdoor scent. Worst of all, the pillow was hard and lumpy. Tamara burrowed deeper into its depths, but it was really impossible to get comfortable.

"If you don't stop that infernal squirming, my brotherly attitude is going to undergo a radical change, sweetheart." Brody's amused voice reverberated beneath her ear.

She was so deeply enwebbed in sleep it didn't even surprise her to discover that her pillow was Brody's hard, muscular chest and that the car was now parked in front of the white picket fence that bordered Aunt Elizabeth's house.

She lifted her heavy lids and noted inconsequentially that his lean jaw was already faintly shadowed. She wondered idly if he were one of those men who had to shave twice a day. He probably was, she thought, faintly annoyed. The man was almost aggressively masculine.

"Your blackmail isn't going to do you any good, you know," she murmured drowsily. "I'm not going to sleep with you."

She felt his lips brush the top of her head as he chuckled. "You've already slept in my arms. How big a step is it to sleep in my bed?" Then, before she could reply, he put her back into her own seat and opened the door. "Sit still."

He was around the car and opening the door in seconds. To her surprise, instead of helping her out of the car, he scooped her up in his arms and strode down the flower-bordered walk to the front door. After the first startled moment of protest, she lay docilely in his arms. If Brody wanted to act the macho male, she wasn't going to protest. Besides, she was finding it extremely difficult to keep her head from nodding once more onto that warm, solid chest.

After he'd set her gently on her feet on the porch, he took her evening bag, extracted the key, and deftly unlocked the door. She was almost asleep on her feet as he took her once more in his arms and held her for a long, peaceful moment. His hand stroked her dark hair gently.

"Is it true what Celia called you?" he asked suddenly. "Are you illegitimate?"

She felt a thrill of shock jar her abruptly awake. She lifted her head warily. "Yes, it's quite true. I'm not only illegitimate, but my mother deserted me a few months after I was born. I don't have any idea who my father was. Does it matter?"

"Yes," he said simply. "I'm glad you don't have anyone else. It makes you more mine. I told you I was very possessive."

"I have Aunt Elizabeth," she protested.

"Ah, yes. I'm beginning to be very grateful indeed for dear Aunt Elizabeth," he said, slightly mocking. "Now close your eyes, sweetheart. I'm not accustomed to behaving like a big brother, and I'm feeling the strain. I want something for myself."

He didn't wait for her to comply before he swooped down and enfolded her in an embrace that was anything but brotherly. Holding her to the strong muscular column of his thighs, he covered her lips with his in a kiss that was almost bruising in its passionate intensity. From drowsy security, Tamara was flung headlong into a blaze of flaming need that turned her both boneless and mindless in his arms. His lips left hers to move hotly in a series of quick, fervid kisses that followed the line of her cheek to her ear, and then returned to ravish the softness of her parted lips as if they were starved for the taste of her. He coaxed her lips open and captured her tongue in his mouth, sucking at it for a long, breathless moment with a hunger that caused her to melt against him with a little moan of sheer animal desire.

Then, before she could recover from this blinding attack on her senses, he put her away from him. His breathing was hoarse and ragged as he opened the door behind her, pushed her inside with a playful swat on her derrière, and said thickly, "I can't take any more right now. You not only go to my head but to other portions of my anatomy that have a decided will of their own. I'll see you tomorrow at eleven."

Without waiting for a reply, he turned and ran lithely down the porch steps, leaving her to gaze after him.

By the next morning Tamara had firmly convinced herself that Brody's mesmerizing effect on her had been engendered purely by the bizarre combination of events and emotions of the evening. She'd obviously been shaken to the point that her imagination had magnified both his powerful charisma and her own response to it. In the clear light of day, when she had time to assess the violent changes that her calm, orderly existence had undergone, she was quite sure she would regain her cool, businesslike reserve and be able to deal with him in her usual efficient, emotionless manner.

She'd reached this conclusion in the wee hours of the morning after lying in bed mentally berating herself for the docile way she'd accepted both Brody's so-called bargain and his lovemaking.

Why had she let him bluff her as he had done?

Now that she was away from that bold, magnetic charm, she could see he had no real weapon to use against Aunt Elizabeth. She had no doubt Margaret Bettencourt would vouch for her aunt's integrity if it came to a confrontation. Though Brody might cause a little unpleasantness if he chose to go to the authorities, she was sure no criminal action could come of it.

No, she'd been so upset by the events of the evening that she'd let him bulldoze her into a commitment that was totally unnecessary. In the morning she'd tell him what he could do with his threats and his blackmail, she thought crossly. With this grim resolve, she forced herself firmly to fall into a sleep that was both restless and short-lived.

She finally admitted that her nerves were too on edge for her to rest properly and dragged herself out of bed and into the shower when the clock on the nightstand read only eight. The cold needlepoint spray brought her to life with shocking rapidity, and she was soon feeling alert and much like her usual cool, confident self as she dressed in her favorite old faded jeans and a lavender cotton shirt.

She made her way briskly downstairs and into the kitchen, only to find a note from Aunt Elizabeth on the kitchen table, propped against an enormous ebony bowl full of golden irises.

Darling,

I thought I'd let you sleep in after your late night. Mabel asked me to breakfast before church, and I'll be having lunch with Reverend Potter afterward. There's tuna salad in the refrigerator for your lunch. Have a good day.

E.

Tamara touched one of the blooms with a delicate finger while she toyed with the idea of going on to church herself, ignoring that the arrogant Mr. Brody had stated he'd arrive at eleven without even asking if it would be convenient for her. No, she would wait for Brody to put in an appearance and give herself the pleasure of telling him off.

She had opened the refrigerator door and was reaching for the pitcher of fresh orange juice when she heard the front door buzzer. With a puzzled frown she closed the refrigerator and hurried down the hall. This couldn't be Brody yet. It was only eight-thirty and he'd clearly said he'd arrive at eleven.

Celia Bettencourt was standing on the top step dressed faultlessly as usual in designer jeans and a Ralph Lauren polo shirt. She started speaking as soon as Tamara opened the door. "I know you have the right to be angry. If it were I, I'd probably slam the door in my face," she said desperately. "But I'm asking you to listen to me. Will you do that?"

"I don't think we really have anything to say to each other," Tamara said coldly. "You made yourself more than clear last night."

Celia moistened her lips nervously and Tamara noticed she didn't look at all well. There were dark shadows under her eyes and her mouth was taut and strained. "I want to apologize for that," she said haltingly. "I know my behavior was unforgivable." She grimaced. "Even if I wasn't aware of it before, I assure you my father let me know in no uncertain terms how disgracefully I'd treated you."

"I'm not in the mood to be very forgiving at the moment, Celia," Tamara said. "There are some things that take a good deal of time to forget before—"

"Look, do you think this is easy for me?" Celia burst out. "Do you think I'd be here if there were any way I could get out of it? I have to talk to you, damn it!"

So much for Celia's abject apology, Tamara thought grimly. "You might as well come in," she said, moving aside reluctantly. "Though I don't agree we have anything to talk about now that you've done your duty. I promise I'll let your father know you've done the proper thing."

"My father doesn't know I'm here," Celia said, stepping hurriedly into the hall as if she were afraid Tamara would change her mind. "I left before breakfast this morning. I wanted to try to see you before my father called you with his own apologies."

Tamara shook her head doubtfully but turned

and preceded her into the living room. "Sit down," she invited curtly, gesturing to the couch while she dropped into the pale blue armchair.

Celia gazed curiously about the room, and she looked no more at home than Brody had with the mellow period furnishings. Tamara stiffened defensively, expecting some caustic comment, but she was startled to see a curiously wistful expression on the other woman's face. "This is nice," Celia said softly. "It's almost like a Norman Rockwell print."

"You like Norman Rockwell?" Tamara asked, surprised. She wouldn't have thought a woman as worldly-wise as Celia would embrace Rockwell's down-to-earth hominess.

But Celia was nodding. "I have several in my room," she said absently. Then she sat up arrow-straight, her thin figure tense. "I want you to go away," she said abruptly.

"I beg your pardon?" Tamara's eyes widened in shock.

"I have some money I inherited from my mother's estate," Celia said, moistening her lips nervously. "It's not a great deal but it's enough for you to resettle comfortably in another town. Perhaps if you're careful you'd even have enough to open your own boutique."

This was the second time in twenty-four hours she'd been offered a shop of her own, Tamara thought wryly. If it hadn't been so insulting, it would have been a little amusing. "I think you'd better leave, Celia," she said, a thread of steel in her voice.

Celia ran her hand through her hair, disturbing her elaborate crown of curls. "Oh damn, I knew I'd make you angry," she said and, incredibly, her brown eyes were glistening with tears. "Look, I know you must hate me as much as I do you, but you've got to listen to me. Can't you see what an opportunity this would be for you?" She bit her lip as Tamara continued to gaze at her without speaking. "All right, give me just a year. Go away for a year and you can still have the money."

"I don't want your money, Celia," Tamara said, shaking her head in bewilderment. "And I don't hate you." Her lips twisted bitterly. "After last night, I can't say you're on my list of favorite people, however."

"I went a little crazy last night," Celia admitted hesitantly. "I saw you dancing with Todd and the way he was looking at you, and I guess I drank a little too much."

"That makes two of us," Tamara said. "I wouldn't have responded quite so readily to your charming little remark if I hadn't had more than I could handle." She shrugged. "Let's just try to forget about it, Celia."

"I can't," she said, her lips trembling. "I can't take any more. Won't you please go away?"

The woman was actually pleading with her. Where was that brittle, sophisticated façade with which Celia Bettencourt usually faced the world? She looked more like a desperate little girl with those big brown eyes swimming with tears. Here was a Celia Tamara had never seen before.

"This must mean a good deal to you," she said slowly, her gaze fixed on the other woman's face. "You don't have to worry about Todd and me, you know. There's really nothing between us."

"Yes, I know that." Celia smiled bitterly. "I also know that Todd wants you. It was clear to everyone at the party last night. You only have to reach out your hand and gather him up as you do all the other prizes."

"Prizes?"

"Even when we were children in school, you were always the bright little star pupil who won all the blue ribbons in sight," Celia said. "And when Daddy hired you after you graduated, he could never stop raving about you. I thought after high school I'd go right into the store but Daddy sent me to Switzerland instead." She drew a deep, shaky breath. "Then when I came back you were even more deeply entrenched."

Good Lord, how close Aunt Elizabeth had come to the truth, Tamara thought with a touch of remorse. Why couldn't she herself have seen beyond that hard stinging exterior to the hurt that lay beneath the surface?

"Why are you staring at me like that?" Celia asked impatiently. "Why don't you say something?"

"I was just thinking that there's so much more

to all of us than what appears on the surface," Tamara said quietly. "And how seldom we make the effort to see beyond the superficial. Do you really love Todd Jamison, Celia?"

"Yes, I really do," the other woman answered simply. "And I can make him love me. Give me a year and he'll forget you ever existed."

"And my job at Bettencourt's?"

"At least I'll have a chance to prove myself to Daddy without standing in your shadow." Her face brightened hopefully. "You're considering it, aren't you? You're going to take the money?"

Tamara shook her head. "No, I don't want your money," she said as she rose to her feet. "But that doesn't necessarily mean you won't get what you want. I'll think about it, Celia."

Celia also stood up. "I suppose I should be grateful you haven't given me an outright refusal," she said, attempting to smile. "I can't lie and tell you I'll like you any better if you do this for me. You've been a thorn in my flesh far too long for me to promise that."

"You haven't made my life exactly a bed of

roses either," Tamara said dryly, as she followed Celia to the door.

"I felt I was entitled to get a little of my own back," Celia defended herself. "That's why I turned Rex Brody loose on you last night." There was a ghost of a catty smile tugging at her lips. "I wanted to see how you'd cope with a man the caliber of Brody. I even told him you'd only gotten the job at Bettencourt's because you'd had an affair with my father."

"Charming," Tamara said sarcastically. "I think perhaps you'd better leave while you're still ahead."

"I didn't really mean to cause—"

"Good-bye, Celia."

The other woman shrugged as she opened the door. "You'll let me know what you decide?"

"Somehow," Tamara answered. "But I don't think either one of us would really enjoy another *tête-à-tête*."

Celia Bettencourt nodded. "Good-bye, Tamara." The door shut quietly behind her.

Tamara shook her head ruefully as she turned and slowly walked through the house and out the kitchen door, instinctively heading for the familiar haven of the greenhouse. There had been a flicker of triumph in Celia's face before she'd closed the door that caused Tamara to bristle instinctively. She doubted if it would ever be possible for her to really like her employer's daughter. Despite the surprising vulnerability Celia had revealed today, there was a little too much of the feline in her demeanor for her to be very appealing. She had an idea Celia would be very disappointed if she realized just how grateful Tamara was feeling toward her at the moment.

As she walked slowly through the garden, she paused for a moment to watch a gorgeous orange and sable butterfly flitting among the marigolds bordering the red brick path. So lovely. So graceful and free as it spread its brilliant wings in the sun.

Flitting. Tamara's lips curved in an involuntary smile. That was how Aunt Elizabeth had described her mother when she'd first explained Tamara's illegitimate birth and her mother's desertion. Carla Ledford had been like a beautiful butterfly that flitted from flower to flower, only pausing to drink the nectar before continuing dizzily on its giddy flight. It wasn't the nature of the butterfly to ponder and worry or to stay in one place, Aunt Elizabeth had told Tamara gently. So one mustn't blame either the butterfly or the flower, but accept it as the nature of things. For years after that explanation, whenever Tamara had seen a butterfly she'd thought of her mother, and the simile had relieved her of any corrosive bitterness she might have harbored.

Aunt Elizabeth saw everything with such clarity and honest simplicity. Tamara had been raised to face life with strength and that same honesty, but now she was forced to acknowledge she hadn't even been honest with herself. As she'd sat watching Celia and thinking how seldom people and actions were what they really seemed to be, she'd suddenly realized what had provoked the scene at the party.

There had been a growing restlessness within her for years that had culminated in that explosion the night before. She must have been mentally rebelling for some time against the emotional and physical strictures she'd placed on herself. Why else had she let Celia's petty shrewishness prey on her nerves after a lifetime of ignoring it? And why had she worn that crimson gown after years of dull anonymity? Now that she looked back on it, her actions had been as smooth and consistent as if she'd formulated them. Celia, Todd, and Brody may have acted as catalysts, speeding up the process, but they were only that . . . catalysts. She was responsible. She *wanted* to break free.

Tamara shook her head in wonder, her gaze still fixed absently on the butterfly. Freedom. It was all so clear now. She'd never have acceded to Brody's blackmail threat so readily if she hadn't subconsciously wanted to go with him. He'd suddenly appeared on her horizon like a bold eagle and she'd instinctively recognized and desired the freedom he represented.

Perhaps there's a little butterfly in the most sedate of us, she mused, as she once more started toward the greenhouse. We hide in our little cocoons until it's time to shrug off the protective confines and try our wings. Going with Brody on his tour might be considered a bit reckless for a fledgling butterfly like herself, but she suddenly knew there was no question that she would do it. The challenge he'd thrown at her was just too tempting to resist. Why shouldn't she begin her new, more colorful existence with a brief, dizzying flight that would break her free once and for all from her cocoon? Yes, she would definitely go with Brody and let that wild eagle show the butterfly how to fly.

She certainly should have no qualms about making use of him after his blackmail attempt. But it probably would be much wiser not to let Brody know she actually wanted to go with him now. Yes, she'd let him think he'd bulldozed the poor little small-town girl into going with him. It would fortify her position and she guessed she might need that strength with a man as forceful as Brody.

There was a smile of infinite satisfaction on her lips as she opened the door of the greenhouse.

Some time later Tamara looked up absently from the pot of bay leaf she was transplanting into larger pots as the door was thrown open. Rex Brody stood in the open doorway with a frown of angry impatience on his face. When he caught sight of Tamara on her knees, contentedly working with her plants, the impatience turned to positive fury.

He kicked the door shut with his foot before striding forward to tower above her intimidatingly. "Do you realize I've been ringing your bell and banging on your door for the past ten minutes?" he grated between clenched teeth. "Since there was a car parked in the driveway I was afraid something had happened to you, so I let myself in. I search all over this Victorian monster of a house, and I finally find you playing in the dirt like a seven-year-old!"

She stared up at him belligerently, striving not to notice how the black jeans hugged with loving detail the solid line of his thighs. His blue shirt was open at the throat, revealing the start of the springy dark hair on his muscular chest. "I didn't hear you ring," she said defensively.

"I'm aware of that. How could you hear me when you were out here making mud pies?" he said caustically. "Why in hell weren't you inside waiting for me?"

Tamara slowly picked up a towel and wiped her muddy hands on it, wishing it were his immaculate chambray shirt. "I'm not in the habit of sitting in the front parlor waiting meekly for visitors like a Victorian miss," she said coldly. "And I'm not making mud pies. I happen to be working. I didn't notice the time, or I wouldn't have been so discourteous as to keep you waiting."

He looked impatiently at the gold watch on his wrist. "I'll give you just thirty minutes to get cleaned up and finish packing," he growled. "As it is, we won't get into New York until late afternoon."

"Are you crazy?" she asked indignantly. "I have no intention of going anywhere today. I have arrangements to make, and I can't waltz off with you without discussing things with my aunt. I may have agreed to your terms but you can't expect me to simply pick up and leave.

You'll just have to give me your itinerary and I'll join you when it's convenient."

He closed his eyes and drew a deep breath. She could feel the waves of anger that were radiating through his motionless body, and when his eyes flicked open, they were blazing with dark fire. "I'd advise you not to goad me today, Tamara," he said, enunciating very precisely. "I was mad as hell at you before I even arrived here, and this little game of hide-and-seek hasn't improved my temper. In addition to my less than indulgent mood, I'm in a hurry, damn it!"

"It's hardly my fault you got up on the wrong side of the bed this morning," she said, glowering at him. "And I'd appreciate it if you'd refrain from blaming me for your own bad temper."

"The hell it wasn't your fault," he said roughly. "After I left you last night, I went back to the party and had a little chat with Todd Jamison."

Her eyes widened in surprise. "I'm amazed that he was capable of discussion," she said. "He could barely stand up when I last saw him."

"He was not only capable, he was positively verbose," he said darkly. "Once he got started, I couldn't shut him up. He wasn't just lyrical about your 'talents,' he was quite explicit."

Tamara could feel the warm color dye her cheeks scarlet and she dropped her gaze, her long lashes dark shadows on the curve of her cheeks. "That must have given you a kinky little thrill," she said scornfully, lifting her eyes again to glare at him.

"You could say that." His lips twisted painfully as his gaze moved compulsively over the voluptuous curve of her breasts, clearly outlined in the faded lavender shirt. "I couldn't decide whether I wanted to wreak havoc on Jamison or you. I didn't get to sleep last night thinking of you in bed with that loud-mouthed bastard, letting him do all those things to you. I wanted to do everything with you that he'd done and more. I wanted to wipe your mind free of every other man who'd ever touched you."

A wave of heat flowed over her, tuning her body to an exquisite sensitivity. He wasn't even touching her, yet the intensity of that look and the erotic picture his words evoked caused a strange, melting sensation in her loins. "How very chauvinistic of you," she said a little shakily, as she attempted to meet his dark gaze that was flickering now with desire as well as anger.

He scowled. "Perhaps I am," he admitted. "I know I don't have any right to question your past. I've never been an angel myself where women were concerned. I shouldn't care how many men you've had." Then his face darkened and his hands knotted into fists. "But damn it, I do! I don't want to meet another man who's had you, and if you ever let anyone else so much as lay a finger on you, I'll probably tear him apart."

She shivered as the absolute sincerity in his tone came home to her. Then she lifted her chin defiantly as she realized he was doing it again! Despite all her resolutions, Brody was manipulating her emotions and intimidating her just as he'd done last night.

"I can't say I'm interested in either your sexual fantasies or your possessive delusions, Mr. Brody," she said icily. "And I certainly don't intend to indulge you by paying the slightest attention to any strictures you attempt to place on me. I run my life as I see fit."

"Rex, damn it," he bit out. "And you'll be very interested in my sexual fantasies in the near future, I promise you." He drew a deep breath and ran his hand through his crisp dark hair. "But all that isn't important right now. I have to be in New York by late this afternoon, and you're coming with me. Now, let's get moving."

"Perhaps you didn't hear me. I can't possibly leave today," Tamara said. "So I'd suggest you leave without me."

"Of course you can leave today," Rex asserted arrogantly. "All you need is a little organization. Now—what do you have to do?"

Tamara sighed resignedly and counted slowly to ten. She spoke with painstaking slowness as to a very young child. "I have to discuss my plans with my aunt. I have to pack. I have to give at least a week's notice to Mr. Bettencourt, and I have to find someone to care for my plants while I'm gone."

He frowned impatiently. "I'll help you pack. That shouldn't take long. You can call your aunt from New York and explain. You don't have to worry about Walter. I told him at breakfast I was taking you with me today."

"Wasn't that a trifle presumptuous of you?" she asked angrily. "I owe the store at least a week's notice, and it was my place to speak to my employer."

"I was hoping to spare you the awkwardness of what I assumed would be a painful situation." His voice was dangerously soft. "I'd forgotten how close you once were. Perhaps you wanted to bid him a fond farewell."

"As you're quite sure I have the morals of an alley cat, you may find it difficult to believe I have other motivations in my relationships with men other than luring them into bed with me," she said caustically, rising to her feet. "I owe Mr. Bettencourt a great deal. It's only courteous to give him notice personally."

Rex's lips twisted cynically. "I wouldn't worry about that if I were you. I got the distinct impression that Walter was quite relieved not to have to speak to you. I gather that Celia was almost hysterical last night after you stalked out of the ballroom like a disdainful princess. I think it will be much more comfortable for Walter this way."

"I guess you're right," Tamara said, a trace of bleakness in her violet eyes. "Perhaps I'd better take you up on the offer of that boutique on Rodeo Drive. I don't imagine Rex Brody's latest mistress will be very welcome in Somerset."

Rex frowned again. "The whole world doesn't revolve around this little Peyton Place, you know. I promised I'd protect you."

"The world might not, but Aunt Elizabeth's life certainly does. For that matter, so has mine for almost twenty-three years," she said.

"I told you I'd make everything right for you."

"There are times when you can't just wave a checkbook and have everything fall into place."

"Thanks for the vote of confidence," he said ironically. "I think I can demonstrate that I have a few more assets than the ones in my bank account." He gestured impatiently. "Now that we've disposed of your arguments, shall we start packing?"

She shook her head decisively. "Even if I agreed with your rather arbitrary disposal of my other objections, I still have no one to care for my plants."

He gave the interior of the greenhouse a cursory glance. "Surely your aunt could water your flowers for you," he said carelessly.

"Plants," she corrected firmly. "And they require a good deal more attention than watering. I've spent two years developing and nurturing some of these strains, and I'm not about to forfeit all my work by putting someone in charge who has little or no knowledge of horticulture. You'll have to wait until I can hire a competent person. What can a week matter?"

"It matters," Rex said grimly. "Let me get this straight. You won't come with me because you haven't got someone to babysit a bunch of plants?"

"I'm delighted I've finally gotten through to you," Tamara said with a demure satisfaction she didn't bother to conceal. "That's exactly what I mean. So you'll just have to do without me until I'm free, won't you?"

"Like hell I will!" he said explosively. He turned and strode out of the greenhouse, slamming the door behind him with a violence that caused the glass panels to vibrate.

Tamara flinched involuntarily. It seemed the forceful Mr. Brody wasn't at all pleased on the odd occasion when he didn't get his own way. Well, he'd just have to become accustomed to it, because she was through jumping whenever he snapped his fingers. There was a serene smile on her face as she once more picked up her trowel and began to work.

FOUR

TAMARA WORKED CONTENTEDLY at her gardening for the remainder of the day, resolutely blocking out the thought of anything that even remotely reminded her of either Rex or the upsetting events of the last twenty-four hours. In fact, she was so successful that it came as a tiny shock when Aunt Elizabeth called her for the evening meal, and she realized it was nearly sundown. She quickly checked the thermostat on the wall and hurried out of the greenhouse and across the backyard to the house.

Aunt Elizabeth, looking trim and youthful in blue jeans and a neat white blouse, was at the stove stirring a concoction that smelled gloriously appetizing.

Tamara gave her a fleeting kiss on the back of her neck as she went by. "I'll be with you in fifteen minutes, love."

"No hurry. It's only soup and sandwiches tonight. I knew you'd need to shower so I called you a bit early."

It may have been only soup and sandwiches but when Tamara sat down at the kitchen table opposite her aunt some thirty minutes later, the meal looked mouthwateringly delicious. Crusty, golden homemade bread, thinly sliced ham and roast beef, and Aunt Elizabeth's vegetable soup which was always sheer ambrosia.

"Absolutely fabulous," Tamara said enthusiastically as she helped herself to sliced tomatoes from the blue willow platter.

"Hunger makes the best sauce," Aunt Elizabeth quoted, then she frowned. "I see you didn't touch the tuna salad."

"I forgot," Tamara murmured guiltily.

"You always do." Her aunt sighed. "You'd

starve to death if there weren't someone around to remind you to eat."

"Well, you *are* around," Tamara said, grinning. "And you can't say I'm not a healthy specimen. Did you enjoy yourself at Reverend Potter's?"

"Oh yes, it was very pleasant," Aunt Elizabeth said vaguely, still gazing at Tamara with a frown. "I do hope that young man makes sure you eat properly."

Tamara's hand, in the act of reaching for the ladle of the soup tureen, froze for a brief instant in midair before completing the action with careful precision. "Young man?" she asked casually, lowering her lashes to veil her eyes. "What young man?"

"Why, the one with the music, dear," her aunt said matter-of-factly. She lifted her spoon to her lips and tasted the soup, and a pleased smile lit her face. "I tried a dash of paprika in this recipe tonight. I believe it gives the soup a nice lift."

Tamara sighed as she put the ladle back in the tureen and looked up to meet her aunt's serene gaze. At times there were definite disadvantages to living with an honest-and-true psychic. "Okay, Madame Zara, how much do you know?"

"Oh, not very much, dear," Aunt Elizabeth said. "It wasn't a complete revelation, you know. It was more of a very muddled, fleeting impression. When are you going away?"

"In about a week," Tamara answered cautiously. She'd decided there was no way she was going to burden her aunt with the entire story that led to her acceptance of Rex's proposal and she'd constructed a half-truth she hoped was fairly plausible. "I decided I'd like to try something new, so I resigned from Bettencourt's and I'm going to take a temporary clerical position touring with an entertainer. It will only last a month and then I'll return and consider my other career options." She smiled brightly. "I have a little money in the bank. Perhaps I'll just take a few months off and work on my book."

"A week? I received the impression that it would be much sooner than that," Aunt Elizabeth said, frowning. Then her face cleared

Iris Johansen

and she added, "Oh well, perhaps I was mistaken. What's the young man's name, dear?"

"Rex Brody," Tamara answered. "He's Margaret Bettencourt's nephew and evidently very well known. It will only be for a short while and I'll be perfectly safe. You mustn't worry, darling."

"Oh, I'm not worried," her aunt assured her tranquilly. "I have nothing but good vibrations about this move of yours, dear." A tiny frown wrinkled her brow. "Though there was some disturbance about the blood."

"Blood?"

"Oh, it was all quite mixed-up. There's nothing to worry about I'm sure," Aunt Elizabeth said comfortingly. "It was just a bit puzzling. I'm certain all the details will come in much clearer next time."

Tamara hoped ruefully that some of the details would remain permanently blurred. How could anyone hope to practice even a well-meant deception when her aunt knew more than she did about her own future?

"I'll call you as soon as we arrive in each city,"

Tamara said gently. "You won't be too lonely, love?" It was the first time they'd ever been separated and Tamara was already feeling a bit misty about the parting.

Her aunt shook her curly white head briskly. "I'll miss you, of course, dear, but I don't believe I'll be lonely." Her blue eyes twinkled. "You're very lucky, you know, Tamara. There's such *music* in that young man!"

"Music?" Tamara asked, puzzled. "Yes, I believe that he's a very accomplished musician. Janie tells me he's quite a famous composer as well." She shrugged. "I really wouldn't know. He's in the pop field, and I don't really care for that type of music."

"That wasn't the music I was referring to, dear," her aunt said absently. Then before Tamara could question this bewildering statement, her aunt ordered firmly, "Now eat your supper, Tamara. Your soup is getting cold."

Tamara obediently picked up her spoon and applied herself to her meal. From past experience she knew that if her aunt didn't wish to continue a conversation, there would be no moving her. Besides, she was determined to let nothing worry her during this next week. For the first time in years she was free to do exactly as she wished, with none of the responsibilities of her career to worry her. She fully intended to enjoy the respite she'd almost forcibly wrested from Rex.

And who knew what Rex's attitude would be after only a few days with her in his fast-moving world? She would be such an alien! She looked musingly around the kitchen with its polished pine cabinets and the red gingham curtains at the window. It was all so simple and homey, and it must be as far removed as another planet from Rex's luxurious surroundings in New York. Back in his own world, populated with the alluring, sophisticated women he was accustomed to, he would probably forget about this temporary aberration over her. She might not even hear from him again once he realized how very far apart they were in every way that really mattered. Of course he was gone for good!

Why did that realization bring this curious flatness? The trip with Rex was merely going to be an interesting interlude before she began her own personal renaissance. It couldn't be disappointment she was feeling, she assured herself quickly. It was just that since Rex's appearance on her horizon, she'd been thrown into a tumult of new sensations and experiences. The very "newness" of the feelings was exciting, so of course it was natural she should feel a trifle confused now that his whirlwind personality was removed from her immediate orbit. In a day or two, when her life was once more on its smooth, orderly track, she was sure she wouldn't give the arrogant Rex Brody another thought.

It was almost noon the next day when the door of her greenhouse swung open explosively and Tamara looked up in amazement to see Rex Brody, dressed in rust-colored jeans and a yellow sweatshirt, stride into the room. Except for the change of clothes, he might never have left, for he still wore the frown of angry impatience that had been on his face when he'd slammed out of the greenhouse twenty-four hours before.

"Do you spend all your time out here?" he demanded, as he crossed to where she was kneeling. He grasped her shoulders and pulled her to her feet.

"Most of it," she answered automatically, staring at him. "What are you doing here? You're supposed to be in New York!"

"I'm very well aware of that," he said caustically. "In eight hours I'm supposed to be onstage at Carnegie Hall and I'm still in this podunk of a town thanks to your blasted stubbornness."

"You mean you haven't been to New York at all?" she asked, her violet eyes widening.

He scowled at her. "How the hell could I go to New York when I've been running around like a madman trying to find this phenomenon of a horticultural expert you insist on?"

"That's why you're still here?" Tamara asked faintly, shaking her head. "That's completely crazy. I told you I'd locate someone and join you later."

"I'm afraid I don't trust you to make that 'later' as soon as possible," he said. "And I want you with me now." Grabbing her hand, he turned and headed for the door, dragging her behind him.

"But I told you—"

"You told me you wanted an expert to babysit your precious plants," he interrupted harshly. "Well, I got him for you, damn it. It took me all day yesterday and a trip to Boston University, but your expert is sitting in your kitchen at this moment. Would you consider a university professor with a Ph.D. in Botany adequate for your needs?"

"Well, yes, of course," she stammered. "But—"

"Well, that's what you've got." He pulled her across the yard and up the back porch steps. "Dr. Lawrence Billings, currently on sabbatical from Boston University and willing not only to make house calls but actually live on the spot and give your herbs tender loving care."

"Live here? But he can't do that! What about Aunt Elizabeth?"

"Why don't you ask her?" Rex opened the kitchen screen door and stepped aside, gesturing mockingly for Tamara to enter.

Aunt Elizabeth was sitting at the kitchen table

beside a tall, lanky man in his late fifties, with iron gray hair and a strong, intelligent face that had no claim to good looks. His gray tweed jacket and dark slacks were well worn but of good quality, and he had an air of careless confidence that reflected the assurance of maturity. He rose at once when Tamara entered the room and his smile was quick and warm.

Her aunt looked up from refilling their visitor's coffee cup and said happily, "Tamara, do stop and say hello to our guest before you leave. Lawrence has just been telling me how eager he is to see your greenhouse. Do you suppose you'll have time to show him around?"

"Yes, of course," Tamara answered dazedly. She wondered just how long ago Rex had arrived. It was clear he'd not only had time to reconcile Aunt Elizabeth to her departure, but for Professor Billings to become "Lawrence."

"I'm afraid that won't be possible, Miss Ledford." Rex's voice contained just the right note of regretful apology. "As I explained earlier, time is of the essence. I'm sure Professor Billings will be more than happy with you as a guide."

"Certainly," Professor Billings agreed genially. "You're extraordinarily well informed for a layman, Elizabeth."

Elizabeth Ledford made a face. "I picked up a little expertise by osmosis living with Tamara, but I'm not in her class."

His keen gray eyes alight with interest, the professor turned back to Tamara. "Your aunt informs me you're writing a book on herbs, Miss Ledford. I'd be very interested to discuss it with you when you're not so rushed. I do want to assure you I'll take very good care of everything while you're away." He smiled ruefully. "I must admit Mr. Brody's offer came like a gift from heaven. My sabbatical actually ended two months ago, but I had the bad luck to contract a rather virulent flu that put me out of action for some time. I was supposed to start teaching a summer course next month, but I'm under doctor's orders not to return to the classroom for at least another six weeks, so Mr. Brody's exceptionally generous terms came just in the nick of time."

"It's all working out so well for everyone,

dear," Aunt Elizabeth said with a beaming smile. "Rex explained how disappointed you were not to be able to accompany him on the first part of the tour. Now, thanks to the Professor, you not only can start your new job right away, but I'll have his company while you're gone. Isn't that wonderful?"

"Wonderful," Tamara echoed faintly. Thank heavens Rex hadn't blown her story about the clerical position.

"I've packed two bags for you, and I'll send the rest of your luggage along to your next stop. Rex tells me that will be Houston," her aunt went on briskly. "Now all you have to do is change and pack your herb bag. I knew you'd want to do that yourself." She turned to Lawrence. "Tamara never goes anywhere without her herb bag. It has everything from herbal medicines to sachets."

"Really? I'd like very much to examine it," Lawrence said. "I did a paper on the history of herbal medicines a few years ago. It's really quite a fascinating subject."

"Yes, it is," Tamara said eagerly. "Particularly the early uses of belladonna. Did you—"

"I hate to curtail your discussion," Rex interrupted smoothly, "but we really must be on our way, Tamara." His iron hand closed on her arm with scarcely veiled impatience. "If you'll excuse us, I'll just accompany Tamara to her room and bring down her suitcases."

"Certainly, Rex dear," Aunt Elizabeth said, giving him a fond glance. What magic had Rex worked on her aunt, Tamara wondered bewilderedly. He had the very independent Elizabeth Ledford practically eating out of his hand. "But do come back down and join us for coffee. I want you to try my sugar doughnuts."

Rex's smile was totally charming. "I wouldn't miss them," he assured her with boyish enthusiasm. "Come along, Tamara."

With his hand under her elbow, he propelled her firmly and quickly from the kitchen and down the hall. They were halfway up the stairs before she was able to jerk away from that steely grasp and turn to mutter crossly, "You don't have to push me, Rex 'dear.'" She stamped angrily ahead of him up the stairs. "I'm well aware I've no choice but to go with you now that you've completely rearranged my life to your satisfaction. Tell me, how did you manage to bamboozle Aunt Elizabeth with all that phony boyish charm?"

He grinned. "I'll have you know my charm is not phony. I'm just a simple, all-American type and your aunt has the good taste to recognize it."

"You're about as simple as a Rubik's Cube," she said grimly, as she opened the door to her room. She threw him a speculative glance. "I suppose it's too much to ask that now that you've met Aunt Elizabeth you'll admit she couldn't possibly be the criminal you thought her?"

"No chance," he replied tersely. He followed her into the room and shut the door. "I'll grant you she's a delightful woman, but that's no sign she's not a crook. When I was a kid, the numbers racket in my neighborhood was run by a little, white-haired old lady who resembled everyone's dream image of a grandmother."

She whirled to face him, prepared to make a scathing condemnation of his cynical attitude. Suddenly she lost track of what she was going to say. Rex stood in the middle of her bedroom, looking as boldly out of place as a pirate in the silken chamber of a lady-in-waiting. His dark vibrance charged the serenity of the room with an electricity that was almost violent. She wondered if she would ever be able to occupy this room without remembering Rex standing here, appraising her with those mocking dark eyes.

She was suddenly overpoweringly conscious of everything about him. The way his thick, dark hairline formed into a slight widow's peak, the rhythmic movement of his hard muscular chest as he breathed, the almost indecent snugness of his rust jeans as they molded the flatness of his lean stomach and hips. She felt a slow heat burn through her that was as potent as it was bewildering.

"Shall I lock the door?" he asked, and her gaze flew up to his in shock. She saw the same sexual awareness that she was experiencing. His dark eyes were hot and intent as they roamed over each valley and curve of her body, and his beautifully sensual mouth was oddly tender. "Let me love you, sweetheart," he said huskily.

She drew a deep steadying breath, angry she'd let him see how his presence aroused her. She felt a languid melting in her loins and braced herself as if for a physical assault.

"No," she said sharply, even as her breasts moved tumultuously with her uneven breathing. She pointed to the two suitcases by the bed. "That's what you came up here for and that's all you're getting, Rex Brody."

For one breathless moment she thought he would ignore her rejection and take her in his arms. Then his body relaxed, and he drew a deep, ragged breath. With a muttered curse he swung away from her, snatched up the bags, and stormed angrily toward the door. "If you're not down in fifteen minutes, I'll take it as an engraved invitation," he said grimly. The door closed decisively behind him.

Tamara gazed at the door, a curious indignation mixed with her relief that Rex hadn't exploited that brief moment of fluid electricity that had leaped so suddenly between them. If he'd held her in his arms, she didn't know if she would have had the will power to refuse his taking anything he wanted of her. She was only grateful she hadn't been put to the test, and she certainly didn't want to face him again in the intimacy of her bedroom. He'd said fifteen minutes and she had a shrewd idea if she wasn't downstairs in that time, he'd have no compunction about coming up to get her.

In ten minutes she'd showered and exchanged her faded jeans and shirt for a tailored cream-colored blazer and matching pants and a peach silk blouse that looked glowingly attractive with her golden skin and shining, blue-black hair. She slipped on bone-colored high-heeled shoes and swiftly put her hair up in a knot on top of her head, leaving a few wispy tendrils to float alluringly about her face. There was no time for makeup, and she hurriedly checked her herb bag to make sure it was fully stocked. Finally she picked up from her desk the bulky loose-leaf notebook that contained her manuscript notes, and tucked it into the bag. She gave the room a last hurried look before closing the door and almost running for the stairs.

Rex met her on the upstairs landing. "You're five minutes late," he said, as he took the bag from her. "I was hoping you'd changed your mind." His eyes lingered caressingly on her flushed face. "Pity."

She shot him a lethal glare and, tilting her nose in the air, sailed down the staircase. Aunt Elizabeth stood in the entrance hall at the bottom of the stairs and drew her into a loving embrace as she reached the last step.

Tamara clutched her aunt's slender form in a tight hug, her eyes filling with tears. Aunt Elizabeth had such quantities of inner strength that no one ever thought of her as being old or fragile, but suddenly Tamara realized just how delicate and vulnerable an old lady she was. "Will you be all right?" she asked huskily. "I don't want to leave you alone."

"Of course I'll be okay, if you'll just refrain from breaking my ribs," Aunt Elizabeth said ruefully, unwinding Tamara's arms from around her and pushing her gently away. She stroked

Tamara's cheek gently. "Don't you dare worry about me, Tamara Ledford," she scolded with tender fierceness. "I won't be alone. I have that nice Professor Billings to keep me company. I managed to take very good care of myself for quite a long time before you were born, and I'm entirely capable of doing it for some years to come." One long finger touched Tamara's wet lashes. "I was lucky to have you to myself for so long."

She looked over Tamara's shoulder at Rex coming with purposeful slowness down the stairs, and leaned forward to whisper mischievously, "You won't miss me for long, dear. When I shook Rex's hand, I realized the music was even stronger than I imagined."

It was the second time Aunt Elizabeth had made reference to that mysterious music, but Tamara impatiently pushed the allusion aside. "I suppose I'm stupid to get so choked up over only a month's parting," she said. "I'll be sure to call you often, love."

Rex had reached the bottom of the stairs and

he grasped Tamara's arm. "I'll take very good care of her, Miss Ledford," he promised.

"I know you will, Rex," Aunt Elizabeth answered serenely. "You won't forget to remind her to eat?"

"If necessary, I'll force-feed her myself," he said lightly.

Tamara felt maddeningly like a small child with all the grownups talking above her and about her but never to her. How dare Rex be so possessive in front of Aunt Elizabeth? And Aunt Elizabeth seemed to accept his assumption of responsibility as a matter of course.

She kissed her aunt on the cheek. "Good-bye, darling," she said huskily. "Take care." Her eyes were glistening with tears as she turned and hurried through the door that Rex was holding open.

Rex didn't speak until he'd settled her in the Ferrari and slipped into the driver's seat. He shot an exasperated glance at her shaking lips and her eyes that were brilliant with unshed tears. "Will you knock it off?" he growled, as he put the car into gear. "I'm not carrying you off to a brothel, you know."

"Aren't you?" she asked shakily.

He glowered at her but didn't respond verbally as the Ferrari roared into motion. Tamara stared blindly out the window at the passing scene and was conscious of a growing sense of unreality as they passed the well-tended grounds and large, red brick building of her old high school, the white steepled church she'd attended all her life. A little over an hour ago she'd been peacefully working with her plants, wrapped in the quiet security of the dear and familiar. Now she'd been ripped away from her old moorings and was caught in the whirling eddies generated by the enigma that was Rex Brody.

She was abruptly awakened from her abstraction when they reached the highway and instead of turning south, Rex headed north.

She sat up straight. "You're going the wrong way," she protested.

Rex shook his dark head as he turned right at a small blue sign lettered McCarthy Airport.

"It would take too long to drive to New York

now. I've lost too much time already so I arranged to charter a plane and have my car driven down later." He made a face. "I had to settle for a prop job. The runways at this private field aren't long enough to accommodate even a small jet."

"What a pity," Tamara murmured. The look Rex shot her, as he brought the sports car to a smooth halt beside a large hangar adjacent to the runway, was definitely intimidating.

As she climbed the steps and entered the cream and gold Beechcraft a few minutes later, Tamara thought a few people would have been quite happy to settle for the unobtrusive luxury of this plane. The passenger compartment seated eight, and the tan and cream tweed-covered seats were grouped for informal comfort, with a polished mahogany writing table between each pair of chairs. The plush rust carpet contrasted with the glowing mahogany paneling, and the small bar at the rear of the plane was built of the same beautifully textured wood.

"Sit down and fasten your seat belt," Rex said as he entered behind her. He turned to the door leading to the cockpit. "I've had the pilot standing by since nine this morning. We should be taking off any minute. I've got to check our ETA in New York and then radio ahead to arrange for us to be picked up at the airport on Long Island and driven into Manhattan." Without waiting for her to reply, he disappeared into the cockpit.

Tamara sat down, opting for an aisle seat rather than a window. The one time she and her aunt had flown from Boston to New York, she'd gotten a bit queasy looking down at the patchwork terrain below. She was fumbling with her seat belt when Rex returned. He brushed her hands away and deftly fastened the belt before dropping into the seat across the aisle from her.

"Take off your jacket and get comfortable. It will be about an hour and thirty minutes before we arrive in New York." Then to her surprise he drew a crumpled sheet of paper and a stub of a pencil from the back pocket of his jeans and proceeded to ignore her. Whatever he was working on, it was receiving his complete attention, Tamara noted, as she slowly pulled her own notebook out of her bag and put it on the table in front of her.

It wasn't until they'd been in flight over an hour that Rex looked up, his face intent and abstracted, to meet her puzzled gaze. The absorption gradually faded and he grinned with an appealing boyishness. "Sorry, I just wanted to polish these lyrics while I had the chance. It's going to be pretty frantic once we reach New York."

"It's a new song?"

He nodded. "I did most of it last night when I was holed up in that motel outside Boston, after I'd contacted Billings and wrapped him up in pink ribbons for you." He made a wry face. "It kind of reminded me of the old days when I was on the road and the only spare time I had to do any composing was either after the show or while I was traveling. Only then I usually went by bus, not plane." He smiled reminiscently. "My first single that went platinum was written on a paper towel from the washroom at the Greyhound bus station in Milwaukee." He folded up the paper he'd been working on and stuffed it carelessly back into his pocket.

"How are you able to compose music without an instrument?" Tamara asked, interested in spite of herself at this glimpse of Rex's colorful past.

He chuckled and reached across the aisle to flick her nose with a playful finger. "You don't, sweetheart," he answered, his dark eyes twinkling. "Even *I'm* not that good. I never travel without my guitar, though I prefer a piano for composing if one is available. My guitar is stored with the rest of the luggage in the cargo compartment."

"I see," she said a trifle crossly, feeling a bit of a fool. How did she know how pop singers composed their songs? Judging by the cacophony of discordant notes that were produced by some of the more famous groups, their music might well be composed on a rusty washboard. She huffily turned her attention back to her own work with the firm intention of ignoring him.

Rex evidently had other ideas, though. He checked his watch, then rose to his feet, stretching lazily. "How about a cup of coffee?" he asked. Without waiting for a reply, he strolled to the bar in the rear of the plane and poured two coffees from a large thermos on the counter. He added cream to one, then returned and offered it to her.

"Thank you," she said, gazing at him curiously. "How did you know I took cream in my coffee?"

"Your aunt mentioned it this morning when she was stuffing me with coffee and sugar doughnuts," he said with a shrug, half sitting on the arm of his chair, his long legs stretched out before him in the aisle. "She seemed to think it was an insult to her coffee-making expertise to dilute the flavor with milk."

Tamara took a sip of the aromatic coffee. "Yes, she would. Aunt Elizabeth is a purist where cooking is concerned," Tamara replied absently. "But isn't that a rather unusual thing to remember about a comparative stranger?"

"Is it?" Rex took a sip of his coffee before looking up, his face surprisingly serious. "But then I don't intend that you remain a stranger,

Tamara. Before I'm through I'm going to know everything about you. I want to know what you love and what you hate and all the in-betweens. I want to know not only what pleases that gorgeous body, but what's hidden behind the mask on that very beautiful face." He reached over to tap her notebook with a forefinger. "For instance, I want to know about this. Is this the book your aunt mentioned you were writing?"

Tamara nodded, her lips curving wryly. "I hardly think you'd be interested in this particular subject. I'm well aware my interest in herbs is definitely esoteric in this day and age. Though, actually, the book also is going to be a sort of potpourri of all the fascinating little tidbits of information I've picked up along the way." Her face lit up with enthusiasm as she warmed to her subject. "The chapter I'm working on now is a complete dictionary of the language of flowers."

Rex grinned. "You mean like giving someone red roses denotes true love?"

"That's probably the best-known one," Tamara agreed with a smile. "But each flower has its own meaning, and some of them are far from complimentary. For example, if someone gives you a horseshoe leaf geranium it means you're stupid, and a hydrangea is a deliciously subtle way of calling you a boaster."

"Ouch!" Rex said with a comical grimace, his ebony eyes dancing. "I can see I'm going to have to pay more attention to the flowers my fans send to my dressing room. They may be trying to tell me something." His gaze fixed on her glowing face. "What other subjects are you going to broach in this masterpiece?"

"Well, I thought I'd throw in a few magical recipes," she said demurely, her violet eyes sparkling. "Like the preparation of an A-one love potion, and an ointment to rub on your broomstick to make it fly."

"Ah-ha, you *are* a witch! I knew when I saw you work on those poor cretins at the party that you were an enchantress. What love potion did you beguile them with, Morgan le Fay?"

"I seem to be steadily going down in your opinion," she protested. "First I was Guinevere and now I'm demoted to the wicked sorceress. In no time at all I'll be kicked out of Camelot."

Rex bowed with panache. "Not as long as I have my sword and mace to defend you, my lady."

"You're doing it again," she said crossly. "What do I have to do to convince you I'm not a throwback to another time?"

"Sorry," he said with an unrepetant grin. "You've got to admit not many modern young women can discuss knowledgeably the language of flowers or know how to brew up a love potion. Since I can't seem to think of you in any other context, I'm afraid you'll just have to resign yourself to accepting me as your knight, pretty lady."

"My black knight, perhaps," she answered, a reluctant smile tugging at her lips. "Your actions toward me to date haven't been guided by any code of chivalry that I've ever read about."

"You haven't been reading the right books," he drawled. "I'm sure in-depth research would reveal those knights in armor were far from reluctant about carrying off a sexy wench across their saddle bow."

"Then I'm sure you'd have been right at home," she said dryly.

A red light suddenly lit up over the cockpit, and a melodious chime sounded.

"You've just been saved by the bell, sweetheart. That's the seat-belt signal. We're starting our descent." He dropped down into his seat and fastened his own seat belt. "Buckle up, honey."

Tamara absently obeyed his instructions after carefully returning her notebook to her bag. She leaned back in her seat, her gaze fixed in surreptitious fascination on Rex's bold profile. Why couldn't she maintain her usual cool air of reserve around the man, she wondered helplessly. One moment she was furiously annoyed and indignant. The next instant she found he'd somehow gotten under her guard and she was not only physically attracted to him, but mentally stimulated by him too. She couldn't deny that in the last thirty minutes he'd completely disarmed her with that puckish humor and his frank interest in her work.

What was even more worrisome was the

vague, insidious pleasure she was beginning to feel in his affectionate protectiveness. Though she'd never lacked for love, thanks to Aunt Elizabeth, Tamara had been taught by both word and example to be strong and independent. This being the case, Rex's unshakable belief that she was a person to be meticulously cared for should have annoyed her. Instead she was finding it very comforting to know she could not only lean on his virile strength, but that she was actually expected to.

The more she learned of the myriad facets of Rex's personality, the more convinced she became that the superstar would prove to be infinitely dangerous. She could guard herself against the sheer sexual impact of his virility, but how could she prevent this strange surge of warm contentment that often flowed through her in his presence?

FIVE

THE PRIVATE AIRPORT where the Beechcraft landed was much larger and busier than the one outside Somerset, Tamara noted, as she watched two uniformed attendants roll metal stairs up to the cabin door.

A long, black, chauffeured limousine was parked several yards away. As Rex ushered her leisurely down the steps, the car's rear door opened and a large, burly man in his late forties climbed out. Though impeccably dressed in an obviously expensive, steel gray business suit, his bearing was that of a marine drill sergeant as he strode toward them. There was a frown of exasperation on his blunt jowly face.

Rex watched his approach with a sparkle of mischievous amusement in his dark eyes. He bent close to Tamara's ear and murmured, "Oops! Now I'm going to get it."

He "got it" almost immediately.

"For heaven's sake, why didn't you cut it *really* close?" the man erupted sarcastically as soon as he was within earshot. "You have a whole four hours before you go on, and you haven't even rehearsed for the past three days, damn it!"

"It's good to see you too, Scotty," Rex said solemnly, his lips twitching. Turning to Tamara, he said, "Tamara, this extremely surly individual is my manager, Scotty Oliver. This is Tamara Ledford, Scotty."

Scotty Oliver raked her with icy gray eyes. "I hope she was worth it, Rex," he said with insulting emphasis, his face still taut with annoyance. "There'll be critics there tonight who would just love to see the golden boy fall flat on his face. You haven't performed in concert for over three years, and you decide to spend the three days before the show screwing some small-town groupie."

Tamara could feel the hot, embarrassed color stain her cheeks as Rex's hand tightened protectively on her arm. His face darkened and his eyes flickered dangerously. "Cool it, Scotty," he said in a low voice. "You have a right to be upset, but keep it between us and leave Tamara out of it."

Scotty Oliver growled a very explicit obscenity, then turned and stalked furiously to the waiting limousine.

"Sorry about that," Rex murmured, a tiny frown wrinkling his brow. "Scotty's been with me since I was a nineteen-year-old kid with just a beat-up guitar and a gigantic ego. He still tends to think of me in those terms at times. But his bark is worse than his bite."

"And am I supposed to meekly accept his insults because he's an old buddy of yours?" Tamara hissed. "It's not enough that the general public will think I'm your latest mistress, you have to expose me to this!"

For a moment there was an odd vulnerability in Rex's dark eyes and he flushed guiltily. Then before she could decipher this reaction, his lips tightened and his expression regained its former impenetrability. "I said I was sorry," he said tautly. "I can promise you it won't happen again."

"Won't it? I'd like to know how you're going to prevent it. Presumably your charming friend is going to accompany us on the entire tour, and he doesn't appear to be the type of person who can be easily intimidated."

"You're right, Scotty is practically irrepressible. If he won't muzzle that vitriolic mouth of his, I'll just have to leave him in New York."

Her gaze flew in startled amazement to his. "But won't you need him?"

"You're damn right I'll need him," Rex said moodily. "This tour will be pure hell without him along to smooth the way."

"Then why?" she asked. "If one of us is to be left behind, surely it would be more practical to release me from our agreement."

He shook his head stubbornly. "No way. You're going, and if Scotty can't be decent to you, he'll be the one to stay behind."

"That ought to make me really popular with the man," Tamara said gloomily.

Rex ran his fingers through his dark hair and glared at her in exasperation. "For heaven's sake, give me a break. I told you I'd protect you and I will."

"I don't want your blasted protection! I want to go back to Somerset and forget you and your precious manager ever existed," Tamara said stormily, her eyes suddenly suspiciously bright.

"Damn it, don't you dare cry!" Rex practically shouted. "I've got enough on my plate without you tearing me up in that particular fashion."

"I have no intention of crying on your shoulder," Tamara said, haughtily lifting her slightly quivering chin. "I'm not in the habit of venting my emotions on all and sundry, no matter what you think. I'm merely very, *very* angry."

Rex muttered an impatient curse. "Don't lie to me," he said. "You've let me see beneath that glossy shell you wear, and I know just how vulnerable you are. You've no more real defenses than a babe in arms."

She was prevented from answering by their arrival at the limousine. The airport attendant had just finished stowing their luggage in the trunk, and she only had time to shoot Rex an indignant glance before she was forced to get into the car, followed closely by that infuriating individual.

As she settled herself on the plush gray seat between Oliver and Rex, she noticed that the manager's expression was as forbidding as when he'd stomped angrily away. Well, in spite of what Rex believed, she wasn't about to let this surly brute's attitude bother her. She composedly looked around the spacious interior of the limousine, conscious all the while of Oliver's sardonic eyes on her face. She was very careful not to let any of her admiration show as she noticed the built-in bar, the television set, and the smoked glass that separated the passenger area from the chauffeur.

"Impressed?" Oliver gibed, after he'd given the chauffeur orders to start.

"Not really," Tamara replied coolly. "I've never cared for limousines. They always remind me of funerals."

Rex made a noise somewhere between a snort

and a chuckle. "That's what I've always told him, sweetheart, but he's a hard man to convince." He lazily stretched his jean-clad legs before him and put a casual arm on the back of the seat behind Tamara.

"You know damn well it's necessary," Oliver said, frowning. "This limousine is as solid as a Sherman tank, and just having George acting as chauffeur is a deterrent. Or have you conveniently forgotten that night in Dallas when we had to take you to Parkland Emergency with bruises and lacerations?"

"That was five years ago," Rex scoffed. "So my fans were a little too enthusiastic. That's no reason for you to go into a tailspin every time I take my own car out."

"You're too damn reckless," Oliver said harshly. "There are too many crackpots out there to take the chances you do. Remember what happened to Lennon?"

Rex frowned. "We've gone into all this before, Scotty. I'm not about to live like a prisoner behind bars just because there's a possibility some psycho may take potshots at me." He grinned crookedly and idly began to play with the wispy curls on the nape of Tamara's neck. "Though perhaps, with Tamara along, I'll give in to your paranoia on this tour. I wouldn't want to chance even the tiniest bruise on this exquisite skin."

Tamara paid no attention to Rex's teasing remark, which was obviously meant to evoke an indignant response from her. Rex and Oliver's almost casual discussion of wounds and fanatical fans and even the possibility of violent death had thrown her into semi-shock. It was the matter-of-factness of the remarks that struck her like a blow. Rex evidently accepted this aspect of his career with the same nonchalance he displayed toward the harvest of wealth and fame it had also brought. A shiver of fear ran through her as she thought of him so badly bruised and cut that he'd had to be taken to the hospital for treatment. The mere idea affected her so intensely she felt physically ill. Why did he continue with a career that could cause such things to happen?

She was grateful neither man noticed the paling of her cheeks and her sudden discomposure.

Rex's teasing comment was met by a startled rejoinder from Oliver.

"You're taking her with you on the tour!" he exploded. "You can't do that, Rex. The arrangements are all made."

Rex was now stroking the back of Tamara's neck as if she were a favorite kitten. "Then make new ones," he said with a lazy grin. "She's going with us, Scotty." Despite the quiet good humor of his expression, there was a thread of pure steel in his voice.

Oliver's face turned ruddy with anger. "Good Lord, Rex, why do you want to take her with you? She'll just get in the way." He gave Tamara a brief, assessing appraisal, causing the color once again to rise to her cheeks. That contemptuous glare might just as well have stripped her naked. "I admit she's a beauty, but you've never felt the need of a live-in woman before. Lord knows there are enough of them willing to tumble into your bed on the road."

"That's enough, Scotty," Rex said, frowning. "I said she was going."

"Okay! But I'll lay odds you're going to regret

it," Scotty growled. "I'll try to alter the arrangements." His lips twisted cynically. "It shouldn't be too difficult since you'll be sharing a bed."

This was too much! Tamara opened her mouth to tell this rude bastard what he could do with his arrangements, when Rex stopped her by placing a warning hand on hers.

"Easy, babe," he said quickly, not looking at her. His dark gaze was fixed with flintlike hardness on Oliver's belligerent face. "I'm going to tell you this once, Scotty, so I'd advise you to listen," he said with dangerous softness. "I don't want to hear you speak of Tamara in that tone ever again. You don't have to like her, but you'll treat her with courtesy and respect or I'll take a great delight in punching your face in!" He suddenly relaxed and grinned with that irresistible, little-boy charm. "We've been friends for a long time, Scotty," he continued coaxingly. "Don't blow it!" He was idly playing with Tamara's fingers. "And you're wrong about the sleeping arrangements. I'd like to have her as close to me as possible, but Tamara will have her own bedroom."

Anger, astonishment, and cautious speculation superseded each other on Oliver's face. "Separate bedrooms?" he echoed. "She's not your woman then?"

There was a curious expression in the midnight darkness of his eyes as Rex's gaze shifted to Tamara's face. It was a strange mixture of mischief, desire, regret, and something else that caused her breath to catch in her throat and her gaze to cling to his as if enthralled. "No, she's not my woman," he said gravely. He lifted her hand to his lips and pressed a lingering kiss in the palm. "She's my lady."

There was a touching gallantry in the way he uttered "my lady" in that honey dark voice. Tamara was instantly reminded of their recent teasing raillery about knights and chivalry, and she felt oddly moved. She was unable to withdraw either her hand or gaze from his, so lost was she in the strangely timeless moment. She was abruptly brought back to earth when Oliver's voice cut through the misty mood like a finely honed razor.

"Charming," he said sardonically. "But not very explanatory."

Tamara quickly withdrew her hand from Rex's and glanced at Oliver. She was instantly suspicious of the change in his demeanor. Before there had been impatience, anger, and careless contempt in his attitude toward her, but this had undergone a transformation—and not for the better. She sensed not only a chilly wariness, but also an almost menacing calculation in him now. She had an uneasy feeling Oliver was going to prove to be a very dangerous antagonist.

Rex chuckled ruefully and shook his head. "You don't have to understand it, you just have to accept it, Scotty. I'm having a hell of a problem understanding it myself." His expression sobered. "Now tell me about that deal you made with HBO to film the show tonight."

For the remainder of the drive, Tamara was completely excluded from the conversation as the two men discussed residual contract clauses and percentages. Despite her dislike for the man, she grudgingly had to admit that Oliver sounded like a brilliant businessman and exceptionally good at his job as Rex's manager. In addition there seemed to exist a respect between the two that obviously was built on a long and mutually satisfactory relationship. As the discussion continued, Oliver appeared to forget his former displeasure with his client and relaxed. He even chuckled a time or two at Rex's wry remarks, and Tamara was amazed to see a glint of warm affection in those icy gray eyes.

She was so absorbed by the interaction between the two men that she scarcely noticed when the limousine turned into the underground parking garage of a towering modern apartment building. At the end of a ramp black wrought iron gates were electronically opened by a uniformed security guard, and the long, black limousine swept like a graceful bird into the parking garage, coming to a smooth halt a short distance from a row of elevators.

She had her first glimpse of the chauffeur when he jumped lightly from the front seat and opened the passenger door.

"How have you been, George?" Rex asked with easy camaraderie, as he got out and helped

Tamara from the car. "This is Miss Ledford. She'll be staying with us awhile. This is George Edgers, Tamara."

"I'm very happy to meet you, Mr. Edgers," Tamara said politely, as she took in the chauffeur's massive proportions, curly, gray-flecked red hair, and wide, breezy grin.

"My pleasure, Miss Ledford," he said with an admiring look. "I'll bring the luggage right up, Mr. Brody." He turned toward the trunk of the car.

"No hurry, George," Rex said absently, as he took Tamara's arm and led her past two more security guards seated at a desk before the elevators. Nothing was said, but Tamara felt the guards' keen appraisal had cataloged everything about her including her shoe size.

"The security in this building appears to be pretty tight," she commented.

"Scotty found the apartment for me. Security was first on his list of priorities," Rex said, making a face. "You'll get used to it."

Oliver joined them as they entered the elevator, and punched the button for the penthouse.

He checked his watch and said, "It's almost four. I've told George to have the car ready at six. Would it be too much to expect you to be on time?"

Rex grimaced, not at all offended. "Save the sarcasm, Scotty. Have I ever missed a show?"

Oliver's lips twisted. "No, but then you've never skipped three days of rehearsals either. How the hell do I know *what* you're going to do these days." He glanced meaningfully at Tamara.

"Relax," Rex said, with a careless shrug. "Most of the music I'm doing tonight is my own stuff. Who should know it better?"

The elevator door whisked open and Rex escorted Tamara across an elegantly decorated foyer to the door opposite the elevator. "Welcome home, sweetheart," he murmured in her ear, as he unlocked the door and threw it open.

It couldn't have been less like her own home, Tamara thought wryly, as she preceded the men. The apartment was sleekly luxurious, as was to be expected from the little she'd seen of the building. The huge, sunken living room was plushly carpeted in a rich cinnamon shade that contrasted beautifully with the creamy beige contemporary furnishings. The focal point of the room was a wide, stone fireplace, fronted by a modular velvet-covered couch with oatmeal and rust throw pillows. The far end of the room was dominated by a lovely, mahogany, baby grand piano. Beyond it was a wall of sliding glass doors on which hung cream curtains with bold cinnamon stripes. There were a number of doors leading off this central area.

Not giving her a chance for a further appraisal of her surroundings, Rex half led, half pushed Tamara toward one of the doors to the left of the fireplace.

"This is your room," he announced as he opened the door. He raised an eyebrow quizzically. "It's a little small. The master suite is much more spacious and you'd find the master most welcoming. Are you sure you won't change your mind?"

A fugitive smile tugged at her lips as her amused gaze drifted around the guest room. It was lavishly decorated in lavender and cream and was at least twice the size of her bedroom at home.

"I think I'll be able to tolerate this without developing too bad a case of claustrophobia," she said demurely.

"I was afraid of that." He sighed. "Well, if you do change your mind, I'm right next door. Scotty is in the guest room across the living room."

"He lives here?" Tamara asked, startled.

Rex shook his head. "He's only staying here tonight. It's more convenient since we'll be leaving for Houston early tomorrow morning. We won't have time to eat until after the show, so if you're hungry you'd better grab a sandwich in the kitchen." His lips curved. "I'd appreciate it if you'd try to be dressed by six or Scotty will be having kittens."

She whirled to face him. "You expect me to go to the concert with you?"

"Of course," he drawled. "From now on we're going to be as close as Siamese twins. Where I go, you go, pansy eyes. Besides, you've never seen me perform. I'm told I'm fairly fantastic in concert, and I'd be a fool not to take the opportunity to impress you." He made a face. "I'm obviously going to need all the help I can get."

"You may be disappointed," she answered. "I'm not very fond of popular music."

"I suspected that. What could I expect of a woman who was clearly born in the wrong century?" he asked gloomily. "I'll just have to rely on my stupendous talent to bridge the gap." Before she could answer he leaned forward and planted a light kiss on her surprised lips. "I'll see you at six." He was gone before she could reply.

She was standing in the doorway gazing bemusedly after him when Scotty Oliver's voice cut across her abstraction. "You must be a very clever young woman, Miss Ledford," he said, his lips twisting cynically. When he'd entered the living room, he'd thrown himself on the couch in front of the fireplace and propped his feet on the ottoman. The laziness of his burly form was belied by the keen, narrowed eyes that were as alert and wary as a cat's.

She half turned to face him, her expression as guarded as his own. "Clever?" she asked.

"Well, you've obviously got Rex panting like a

puppy dog over you, and Rex is a very experienced man where women are concerned. He's been able to have any chick he's wanted since he was a kid, and in all that time I've never yet known him to let a pretty face interfere with his career." He smiled unpleasantly. "Yes, I'd say you're a very smart little cookie, Tamara Ledford."

Tamara could feel her temper flare with the sheer injustice of Oliver's insinuation. "You couldn't be more wrong, Mr. Oliver," she retorted. "But if you think I'm such a threat, why don't you convince Rex to send me back to Somerset?"

"Believe me, I'll be working on it," Oliver assured her grimly. "So don't get too used to the fringe benefits of being Rex's latest toy, honey. Because it's not going to last."

"Fringe benefits?" Tamara asked, puzzled.

"Don't try on that innocent bit with me," Oliver said contemptuously. "One thing you'll learn if you're going to be around here for any length of time is that all of Rex's financial transactions go through me. He may have called his secretary yesterday to take care of the details, but she automatically passed on the bills to me."

"Bills?" Tamara shook her head. "I don't have the slightest idea what you mean."

Oliver pulled a small spiral notebook from his jacket pocket and flipped it open. "One complete designer wardrobe, expense no object. One Lotus sports car. One diamond and amethyst necklace." He closed the notebook with a snap. "The last item is obviously meant to complement your eyes. Not a bad haul for three days' work, Miss Ledford."

"I suppose you have some idea what you're talking about, but I certainly don't," Tamara snapped.

Oliver shoved the notebook in his pocket and, swinging his legs off the ottoman, stood up. "Come off it," he said, squaring his jaw belligerently. "Rex may let you get away with that wide-eyed act, but spare me, please. Rex has always been generous with his little playmates and I've always felt it was none of my business. But you've been a little too greedy for me to stomach." His words were shot at her with bulletlike hardness. "I'm not about to let you take him on a scale like that, and just so you'll know I mean what I say, I'm going to tell you something that will probably hand you a big laugh. I love that kid. I'd have been damn happy to have a son like him. Beneath all that cynicism and toughness he's the sweetest, most decent guy I've ever known." He drew a deep breath, and then continued. "The car won't be delivered until tomorrow, but the other items on the list were easier to obtain. They're in the bedroom. I hope they meet with your approval."

Tamara stared at him in shock for a long moment before she slowly turned and moved like a sleepwalker into the bedroom. She dropped the jacket she was carrying on the bed and turned to the mirrored closet, which occupied one entire wall of the room. She slowly slid back one of the doors.

She gasped involuntarily, feeling vaguely as if she'd been hit in the stomach. The closet was crammed with clothing of all hues and descriptions. Sport things, day dresses, evening gowns, furs, lingerie . . . The list was endless.

"The necklace is in the top drawer of the dresser," Oliver drawled. He was leaning against the doorjamb, watching her. "It wouldn't have done to have just left it lying around."

Tamara slowly closed the closet door and walked numbly to the dresser, opened the drawer, and lifted out a black, oblong, leather box with a Tiffany label. She carefully opened the box and stared blankly at the necklace blazing in barbaric splendor against the black velvet interior. It was the most magnificent piece of jewelry she'd ever seen. The large square-cut amethysts were interspersed with diamonds that were masterly cut and sparkled with a rainbow of colors.

"Would you like to know how much it cost?" Oliver taunted. "I'd be glad to show you the bill. It would save you the trouble of having it appraised."

"No!" Tamara choked. She closed her eyes, feeling dizzy with the tide of fury that was washing over her in red hot waves. Damn Rex Brody. How dare he put her in a position where she could be sneered at by the Olivers of this world? Did he actually think he could buy his way into her bed with these lavish offerings? She wouldn't even admit to herself that her rage was fueled by a queer, poignant pain that he'd thought so little of her he believed she could be bought like a call girl. He had offered her *carte blanche* that first evening, but their relationship had undergone so much in the past three days she'd honestly believed he'd begun to understand her. And to think she'd actually begun to like the man!

She closed the jewelry box with a sharp click, whirled, and strode purposely to the door.

Oliver took one look at her flushed face and blazing eyes and slowly straightened, his own expression wary. "Where are you going?"

She brushed by him as he instinctively drew away from the almost tangible aura of rage surrounding her. "I'm on my way to *strangle* that sweet, decent guy you're so fond of," she said furiously. "And if you're wise, you'll stay out of my way or I just may start with you!"

Ignoring his look of startled alarm, she marched through the living room to the door on the other side of the fireplace, through which Rex had disappeared. Without bothering to knock, she threw the door open and stalked into a room that was almost twice the size of hers. She received a fleeting impression of midnight blue carpet and drapes, and a king-sized bed covered in a contrasting ice blue, before realizing that the room was empty. A door at the far end of the room was open, however, and the sound of a rich baritone voice singing cheerfully drifted from the room beyond. Without thinking, buoyed up by anger, she crossed the bedroom and marched belligerently through the door.

The singing broke off abruptly as Rex looked up from the center of a huge, sunken, marble tub that might well have graced a seraglio. His dark eyes were twinkling mischievously as he drawled, "I know I said I was fantastic, but you didn't really have to rush in here to see for yourself. I'm really much better onstage than in the bath."

At first Tamara was disconcerted at the sight of him lying languidly, like a sultan awaiting his favorite handmaidens, in the sybaritic blue-veined marble tub. She had only a moment to be grateful for the fact that only a disturbing portion of his copper brown, muscular chest with its curly dark hair was revealed above the mountain of suds, floating on the water, before she remembered why she was there.

She impulsively took a step closer. "I won't be around to see you perform in or out of the tub," she said tightly, waving the black leather jewelry box in her hand. "I just came in here to return this."

He picked up a loofa sponge and leisurely scrubbed his chest while his lazy appraisal took in her flushed face, blazing eyes, and general air of barely suppressed rage. "You're angry," he observed calmly, tilting his dark head to grin at her mockingly. "Now what could I have done to deserve that in the past ten minutes?"

Tamara opened the jewelry box, took out the necklace, and held the beautiful thing outstretched before her as if it were a poisonous snake. "Was I supposed to be impressed by this little bauble?" she asked hotly. "Well, I find it as flashy and vulgar as the man who chose it. I have no use for it so I'd suggest you give it to one of your other women." With that she dropped the necklace into the sunken tub and tossed the leather case in after it. She whirled to leave with a feeling of grim satisfaction, only to feel one slender ankle grasped in an iron hand.

"Oh no you don't, princess." Rex's voice was grim. "You're not going anywhere until I get to the bottom of this."

Then, incredibly, she felt her other ankle similarly encircled, and then a strong jerk toppled her backward into the tub! Rex must have released her ankles immediately after that initial yank, for his arms were there to cushion her impact if not her shock as she was immediately immersed in warm, soapy water.

"You're crazy," she sputtered, as soon as she could get her breath back. "I'm fully dressed, for heaven's sake!"

"So you are," Rex said, studying her now sodden, ruined outfit carelessly. "I'd have waited for you to get out of your clothes and join me, but I doubt if you would have accepted my invitation."

"You're damn right I wouldn't!" she said furiously as she struggled to sit up and release herself from his hold. Rex foiled her attempts with effortless ease, and holding her wrists locked before her, he turned her so that her head was resting on the edge of the tub and her body was facing him in a reclining position.

"Now," he said lazily, "isn't this comfy? So much better than you stalking off in icy disdain and me chasing after you, shivering in my birthday suit."

"Will you let me out of here?" she grated between clenched teeth. She'd discovered in helpless frustration that as long as she remained still her head stayed above water, but any sudden movement resulted in her mouth sinking below the surface.

"Eventually," Brody said calmly. "But not until you tell me why I'm suddenly number one on your hit list. I gather it has something to do with the necklace. Didn't you like it?"

"No, I didn't like it," she mimicked sourly. "And I didn't like the clothes and I'm quite sure I will detest the Lotus."

"I see Scotty has been his usual verbose self." Rex sighed. "I'd wanted to tell you myself, in my own time."

"I just bet you did," she muttered, her eyes blazing violet fire. "No doubt you thought I'd be so grateful I'd jump immediately into your bed. Well, I'm not quite the tart you think me, Rex Brody. You can take your gifts and stuff them!"

Rex's forehead knotted in a frown, his lips tightening ominously. "You know, I'm really tempted to drown you," he said conversationally. "What thoroughly unpleasant ideas you get in that beautiful head of yours. I do *not* think of you as a tart, and those little gifts were *not* meant as bribes."

"And how did you expect me to react?" she asked sharply. "Presents on that scale are fairly self-explanatory. You might even say they're traditional."

"So you immediately assume I'm trying to buy your favors like some villain in an old-time melodrama," he growled. "I expected you to have the sense to know I'd never pull a dumb stunt like that. I admit that at times in my past relationships there has been a mutually agreed exchange of commodities, but give me credit for a little insight into your character, Tamara."

"Then why?" she asked, lifting her chin belligerently. "I hardly think Mr. Oliver is correct and you bought that exorbitantly expensive necklace to go with my eyes!"

There was a curiously sheepish look on Rex's face as he guiltily admitted, "Well, actually that comes pretty close. The necklace was something of an afterthought. I got to thinking how your eyes looked that night on the terrace after your tears had made them sparkle like jewels. I just thought amethysts would look sort of pretty with them."

Tamara's mouth dropped open in amazement. There could be no doubt of the sincerity of Rex's answer. There had been an almost childlike simplicity in his reply. "And the sports car and the new clothes?" she asked faintly.

He shrugged. "I wanted you to feel comfortable. You're an exceptionally lovely woman, but the circles you'll be moving in for the next month are fairly affluent." His lips twisted cynically. "There will be plenty of women who'll have their little hatchets sharpened to take the scalp of a gorgeous thing like you. I just thought I'd give you a little extra ammunition. As for the car, it was a form of insurance."

As she continued to gaze at him uncomprehendingly, he sighed and his dark eyes flickered restlessly. "Look, I know how confining it can be to be in the public eye all the time. Sometimes the restrictions it puts on your personal life are enough to drive you bananas. Your own car gives you at least the illusion of freedom. I was afraid if you didn't have some outlet, you'd be more likely to cut and run."

"I see," she said slowly, biting her lip in perplexity. Incredibly, she did understand Rex's rather strange reasoning. Looking back at what she'd recently learned of his lifestyle, it would seem perfectly logical to him that she would be as upset by the lack of freedom as he was himself. "But isn't this particular insurance a trifle extravagant?"

"Perhaps," he said simply, "but I like giving presents. When I was a kid, we were so dirt poor that neither giving nor receiving presents ever came into the picture. Lord knows I have plenty of money these days, so why shouldn't I give you something?"

Tamara felt a treacherous ache somewhere in the vicinity of her heart, and she found it hard to swallow. Rex's simple words evoked a picture of his deprived childhood and for a moment she experienced an almost maternal tenderness. "But you can't go around giving away sports cars," she said. "It's just not done."

"I was afraid you'd say that," he said gloomily. "I suppose you won't take the necklace, either?"

Tamara shook her head silently, her lips curving in a gentle smile. He looked like a disappointed little boy who didn't understand the insane reasoning of grownups.

"You've got to take the clothes," he argued aggressively, his dark eyes gleaming triumphantly through those almost girlishly long lashes. "How can you protect me from other women if you don't feel perfectly confident and self-assured?" She shook her head doubtfully and Rex pursued coaxingly, "Besides, I bought them all on sale. The stores won't take them back."

Tamara threw back her head and laughed out loud at this outrageous lie. He spoke of the Diors and St. Laurents as if they'd been picked up at a bargain basement jumble sale.

"Lord, but you've a lovely throat," he said suddenly in a husky voice. Reluctantly pulling his gaze away, his eyes lit mischievously. "I've got you, haven't I? You're going to accept the clothes?"

"On the condition that you'll allow me to return them when the tour is over," she agreed hesitantly, wondering at how boyishly pleased he looked at his triumph.

"We'll see," he said evasively. "You're sure you won't take the necklace?"

"No, I will *not* take the necklace," she said firmly, then chuckled helplessly. "Do you realize how totally ridiculous this is? I'm actually lying in a bathtub fully dressed, arguing with you about a dumb necklace."

"It's a very pretty necklace," he defended. Releasing one of her wrists, he groped on the bottom of the tub and triumphantly brought up the glittering piece of jewelry. "If you won't keep it, you can at least let me see how it looks on you."

Without waiting for an answer he sat up in the tub, bringing her with him, and swiftly slipped the necklace over her head. It was surprisingly heavy as it lay in the hollow of her breasts and she looked down at it curiously. Her eyes widened with embarrassment and the color flew to her cheeks. Her breasts might just as well have been naked. Her wet peach silk blouse was clinging lovingly to every curve, and the necklace drew immediate attention to the taut sauciness of her nipples boldly outlined beneath the material.

Rex drew in his breath sharply, and her gaze flew to his face. What she saw there caused her own breath to catch in her throat. His eyes were fixed on the wet, clinging blouse and when he murmured hoarsely, "Damn, that's lovely," she knew he wasn't referring to the necklace.

From playful raillery, the moment had changed to one of unbearable intimacy. Tamara could almost touch the current of electricity that was flowing between them and generating a melting languor in her limbs. For the first time since she had marched through the bathroom door, she was fully conscious of Rex's nudity, of the hard, corded strength of his bronze, virile body that was so different from the satin softness of her own. That he was also experiencing that same violent awareness was evident in the smoky heat of his eyes and the pulse now pounding rapidly in the hollow of his throat.

"No," she whispered dazedly, pulling her gaze by force from that telltale throbbing, knowing her rejection was not aimed at him so much as her own treacherous body.

"Oh yes, sweetheart," Rex breathed raggedly. "Definitely yes!" He drew her slowly and carefully into his arms and she gave a little gasp as the warm hardness of his body seemed to sear through her wet clothing as if it were no barrier at all. She felt his body tremble in response as he pressed her head into the rough thatch of hair on his chest. "We'll have to take it easy, babe." He groaned. "I want you so badly I'm like a kid with his first woman."

She didn't answer, suspended in a sensual

euphoria that consisted of the touch of warm, strong muscles and the rough abrasiveness of the springy hair beneath her cheek. His scent surrounded her and she vaguely identified the piney fragrance of soap and the hot musky odor of the aroused male. The combination was wildly erotic and she suddenly had an irresistible desire to indulge one other sense. Her tongue ventured hesitantly to explore the smooth, corded skin and discovered it was faintly salty. The combination of the taste and the tingling sensation on the tip of her tongue at the contact with his hard flesh was breathlessly exciting. She turned her head, rubbing her cheek against his chest like a playful, sensual kitten as her tongue darted out to stroke teasingly at one hard male nipple.

"Lord!" Rex groaned again, and she felt an almost savage satisfaction at the responsive shudder that shook his body. Then she couldn't think at all as his arms tightened with steely urgency around her, and his mouth swooped down to cover hers in a kiss that wooed and coaxed and tantalized until her lips parted with eager invitation to the invasion of his tongue. She could never remember later how long he explored her lips and tongue in an endless number of hot, breathless joinings. She only knew that with every kiss the aching emptiness of her loins intensified and her blood seemed to run molten fire in her veins, bringing every inch of her flesh to sensitized, vibrant life.

She realized dimly that they were both on their knees now and Rex's usually deft hands were oddly clumsy on the buttons of her blouse. His lips moved from her mouth to her ear and his teeth and tongue alternately nibbled and stroked the lobe. He was murmuring an erotic litany of need and desire, causing such a tumult of sensation within her that she felt strangely weak. She clutched at his strong, naked shoulders as if he were the only rock in a reeling universe. Then the last button was overcome and Rex gently pushed her away to slide the silky material and the flimsy bra beneath it down her arms. He impatiently tossed them over the edge of the tub before feverishly gathering her back to him. The coarse pelt of hair rubbed against her sensitive nipples, engorging them in seconds.

"You are the *softest* woman!" he growled, as his hands ran up and down her naked back, massaging and exploring the graceful line of her spine. "You're all satin and silk and textures." His hands were on her hair now, removing the pins that held her bun in place, and then he threaded his fingers through it as it tumbled down her back in a silken veil. "I love the *feel* of you. Just the way your hair flows between my fingers turns me on."

He pushed her away so that she was leaning against the side of the tub and he caught his breath. His eyes were glazed with passion as they fixed on her full, firm breasts, the dusky pink nipples taut and yearning beneath the barbaric collar of amethysts and diamonds. "I once saw a mural of a long dead Egyptian princess on the wall of a tomb outside Cairo, and I remember thinking she had the most beautiful breasts I'd ever seen." He reached out to cup the warm tempting mounds in gentle hands. "But yours are far lovelier, and you're very much alive."

Alive? The term was a massive understatement, she thought dazedly, as Rex's head bent slowly and he brushed his lips caressingly across the swelling rise of her breasts, leaving a streak of flaming need in their wake. She'd never been so vividly alive in her entire life! Every breath she drew seemed to create new tendrils of sensation, and then his lips moved down to nibble gently at one aching nipple. She made a whimpering sound deep in her throat before she buried her fingers in his crisp dark hair, holding him to her. The cry seemed to excite him unbearably for his hands tightened almost painfully on her breasts. His teeth and tongue worked wildly on the sensitive nipples until she was moaning and writhing beneath him in delicious torment.

"Oh Lord, sweetheart. I'm starving for you." Rex groaned and lifted his head. His lips covered hers with a bruising passion that took her breath away and she was only dimly aware of his movements as he manipulated both their bodies until they were once more lying facing each other. One strong muscular leg slid intimately between her own, making her feel open and vulnerable to attack, and Rex's hands were working deftly at the side fastening of her pants.

When his lips reluctantly left hers for a brief moment, Tamara drew a shaky breath, trying to remember exactly how they'd reached this point. The sudden, physical shock she felt when his hand slid into the front of her pants to caress the curve of her belly brought her to the dreamy realization of the burgeoning of final intimacies. She was so lost, though, in the web of undeniable desire that he'd woven about her that she was almost mindless.

"What are you doing?" she asked hazily, not really caring as long as he kept performing this physical magic that was entrancing her.

He looked up, his warm, loving smile wonderfully reassuring. "I'm trying to get you out of these clothes before I go crazy. I promise I'll make it up to you later, but I've got to get inside you *now,* sweetheart!"

She supposed his frankness should have shocked her, but instead it only served to evoke a mental picture that caused a melting in every muscle of her body. She gazed around her, startled to find they were still in the tub. "But we can't," she protested. "Not here."

"Sure we can," Rex said thickly, as his hand moved around to knead her buttocks with a sensuous rhythm that was both titillating and soothing. "You haven't lived until you've made love in the water. Don't worry, I won't let you drown. There's plenty of room in this tub."

Without waiting for her to reply he lowered his lips to nibble gently at her shoulder, not noticing the sudden stiffening of her body at his words. The casually knowledgeable manner in which he'd uttered that last sentence indicated a wealth of experience that chilled her as surely as if she'd been doused in a pool of ice water. The thought of Rex making love to other women in this very tub made her feel cheap and slightly sick to have been swayed by his sensual magnetism. How could she have been such a fool, she wondered miserably. Then a saving anger surged through her as she remembered how easily he had manipulated her mind and emotions as well as her untrustworthy body.

She tore away from his hold, catching him off guard. As he lifted his head, he caught one glimpse of Tamara's angry white face and blazing eyes before she placed both hands on the top of his head and pushed down with all her strength. He slid underwater like a rock, and Tamara received a distinct pleasure out of keeping him there an instant before releasing him.

Rex came up coughing and sputtering, his dark hair plastered to his head, his eyes streaming with irritation from the soapy water. Tamara had already levered herself out of the tub and was jerkily putting on her blouse when his vision cleared enough for him to see what she was doing. "What the hell was that all about?" he roared.

"I thought you needed to cool off," she said tartly, as she finished buttoning her blouse. She unfastened the necklace and dropped it disdainfully on the floor. "You'd better take this back. You may need it for the *next* idiotic woman you lure into this sultan's pool of yours." She lifted her chin haughtily. "And I'll be more than delighted to accept that wardrobe if it will help prevent some *other* poor simpleton from being taken in by that little-boy charm!" Ignoring both his flushed angry expression and his furious bellow of "Tamara!" she stalked from the bathroom. Her majestic exit was marred by the fact that one of her high-heeled sandals still lay on the bottom of Rex's bathtub, forcing her to limp rather ignominiously.

She was so angry she didn't realize just what an incongruous picture she presented until she passed through the living room on the way to her room.

Scotty Oliver looked up from the magazine he was casually perusing, and his mouth dropped open. He shot up from the couch where he'd been sitting, and his eyes widened as they took in her dripping wet form, shoeless foot, and long dark hair flying wildly about her furious face.

"What the hell happened to you?"

She paused at the door of her room to cast him a glance of infinite dislike. "I decided not to strangle your friend Brody after all," she said icily. "I drowned him instead!" She slammed the door behind her.

Oliver stared blankly at the closed door for a moment before he muttered a panicky curse and bolted for Rex's bedroom.

Six

An hour later, Tamara gazed into the full-length mirror with grim satisfaction. Rex had specified he wanted a glamorous companion as a deterrent—well, she'd sure provided what he'd asked for! The sleeveless gown she'd chosen was of a fine white French wool whose unusual texture appeared richer than satin. The gown was utterly simple, with a low, round neckline revealing the lush beauty of her cleavage. The bodice was loosely bloused and then cinched at the waist with a narrow braided belt of the same material, and the long, narrow skirt was very flattering to the lovely line of her hips and thighs.

In contrast to the simple elegance of the gown, she'd chosen a wrap as barbarically luxurious as any woman could wish. Exquisitely worked silver and gold embroidery played over a field of cerulean blue. The wide, stand-up collar of the wrap formed a breathtaking frame for her face and enhanced the violet of her eyes. She'd brushed her dark hair to a glossy, silken veil and applied a touch of pink lip gloss and a trace of blue shadow to her lids.

She wouldn't have been human if she hadn't been pleased at the difference the beautiful ensemble made in her appearance, and that pleasure helped to alleviate partially the resentment she was feeling both at herself and Rex. The first flush of anger had gradually faded, but she was still filled with an odd hurt mixed with a distinct coolness toward him that she recognized as a bit unreasonable. He'd been perfectly honest about his intentions of luring her into an affair with him, and if she hadn't been so foolish as to be swayed by that potent sex appeal, the episode in his bath would never have occurred. He'd said he wouldn't take her until she was willing, and oddly she had complete trust in his word. She didn't like to admit even to herself how close Rex had already come to reaching his objective. No one could have been more willing than she before he had dropped that remark that shocked her to her senses.

She was a little amazed, though, that the realization that she was just one of a long line of women attracted to the dark fascination of Rex Brody had goaded her into such physical violence. She was discovering new and not altogether pleasant facets of her character since he had appeared in her life. She would never have believed a week ago anyone could so shake her cool control!

Well, she might not have to worry about resisting his future advances. Not many men would still find a woman attractive after she'd not only rejected his lovemaking at a very sensitive point, but had physically humiliated him as well. She'd better prepare herself for a summary dismissal from his life.

Promptly at six there was a brisk knock on her bedroom door and she opened it, bracing herself instinctively for the cold anger she was sure would be awaiting her.

Rex's eyes widened as he took in her dazzling beauty. "Lord, you're gorgeous in that!" he said huskily. His coal dark eyes twinkled mischievously. "Would you accuse me of relegating you to the past again if I tell you that Esther must have looked like you when she first appeared before King Ahasuerus?"

Tamara shook her head. "Actually, I find the biblical reference quite appropriate coming from a man who probably has had as many women as Solomon," she replied tartly. She was experiencing a queer, breathless relief as she detected in Rex no trace of the anger or coldness she'd expected. The realization sent a jolt of panicky dismay through her that immediately brought her guard up.

"Ouch!" Rex said, grimacing. "I don't know if I should be flattered at your assumption of my sexual prowess or insulted you think me so lacking in discrimination. I might remind you that though Solomon had hundreds of women, there was only one Sheba for him." He grinned boyishly. "While we're speaking of biblical references, that was quite a baptism you gave me earlier."

She searched his face but could see nothing but a wry amusement. "You deserved it," she said belligerently. Then, unable to contain her curiosity, added, "Why aren't you angry with me?"

"Believe me, sweetheart, I was furious when you marched out of that bathroom," he said. "But then I realized what had turned you off and I admit to feeling pleased."

"Pleased?"

He nodded. "Yep, I realized I'd evidently made more progress with you than I'd thought if you were showing signs of jealousy."

"Jealousy?" Tamara sputtered, indignant. "Rex Brody, I was not—"

"Scotty is waiting downstairs in the car," he interrupted soothingly, taking her arm and drawing her from the room. "We'll talk about it later, babe."

But once they were in the limousine Scotty Oliver, looking surprisingly elegant in dark evening clothes, immediately engaged Rex in a business discussion that lasted the entire trip to Carnegie Hall. It wasn't until they'd entered the stage door and Rex was about to go to his dressing room that either man again acknowledged her presence.

"I've arranged for Miss Ledford to have a house seat in the third row," Oliver said briskly. "I'll have an usher escort her out front while you check with the orchestra about that change in the arrangement you mentioned."

Rex shook his head. "I don't want her out front," he said flatly. "I want her in the wings where I can see her. Get her a stool and put her someplace where she won't get run over."

Oliver muttered something under his breath, casting Tamara a look of annoyance. "For pete's sake, Rex, she'll just get in the way," he exploded. "Let her sit in the audience and I'll have her brought backstage after the performance."

Rex's lips tightened and his midnight dark eyes turned flint hard. "I want her in the wings," he repeated distinctly. "And I want you to take care of her, Scotty." Without waiting for an answer he turned and strode rapidly down the corridor, leaving a very disgruntled Scotty Oliver gazing after him.

"If you'll just show me where to sit, you can go about your business, Mr. Oliver," Tamara said stiffly. "I assure you I don't want or need either your care or your company."

Taking her by the arm, he propelled her swiftly down the hall. "You heard him," he said tersely, a black scowl on his face. "I'm supposed to watch out for you. I know better than to argue with Rex when he's in this mood." He shot her a bitter, sidelong glance. "You may think you have him as tame as a pussy cat, but you're in for a surprise, Miss Ledford. I've known Rex since he was a tough street kid and that easygoing façade is very deceptive. Beneath it you'll find a layer of pure steel."

Pussy cat? Tamara almost laughed in his face. Of all the facets of his character that Rex had shown her in the past few days, she'd seen no signs of the indulgent tameness Oliver mentioned. Even in his gentler moods, he had the sheathed menace of a playful tiger cub.

"You needn't worry about my underestimating your client," Tamara said dryly. "I assure you I know exactly how tough that street kid can be."

They'd reached the wings of the stage now and Oliver set about finding the required stool for Tamara as well as one for himself. It appeared he had been quite serious about obeying Rex's injunction to take care of her. Tamara was interested in spite of herself in the whirlwind of activity that was taking place backstage. There seemed to be an incredible number of technicians and sound men bustling about, as well as a full orchestra tuning up their instruments onstage.

"There seem to be quite a few people involved in his one-man show," she remarked, as Oliver settled his impressive bulk on the stool next to her.

He gave the scurrying technicians a cursory glance. "It's expected that we provide a little window dressing," he said with a shrug. "But none of it will matter once Rex walks onstage. The audience won't notice anything but him."

"Don't you think you may be a trifle prejudiced in his favor?" Tamara asked skeptically. "He can't be all that good."

There was an odd flicker in Oliver's ice-gray eyes. "Rex said you hadn't ever seen him perform. I thought you were just conning him. But you really haven't seen him, have you?"

She shook her head impatiently. She was getting a bit tired of this incredulous response to her ignorance of Rex's work. "I'm not interested in pop music," she explained crossly. It seemed she'd repeated that quite a bit lately.

Oliver arched a mocking eyebrow. "Tell me that after you see him in action. I'd like to get your reactions after the concert."

"You must be a very good agent, Mr. Oliver," she said lightly. "You certainly believe in the product you're selling."

"I don't have to promote Rex, he sells himself. He's probably the premier performer in the world today. I've never seen anyone generate as much electricity onstage. The man practically carries on a love affair with the audience." As Tamara continued to stare perplexedly at him, he frowned in frustration. "Hell, there's no way I can really define it. You'll see what I mean."

And she did. By the time Rex was doing his last song before the intermission, Tamara was as dazed and enthralled as the wildly responsive audience.

"My word, how does he do it?" she whispered wonderingly, her eyes fixed on the vibrant figure in the center of the stage. He was sitting on a simple stool much like hers, his fingers rippling over the strings of his guitar while his rich baritone notes soared out over the breathlessly quiet audience. She could see what Oliver meant about Rex not needing props. They would only detract from the magnetism he exuded. Even his clothes were simple. His fitted, black suede pants hugged his muscular thighs and his white shirt with its long, full sleeves reminded her vaguely of a pirate's romantic garb. The top few buttons of the shirt were left open to reveal the corded, hair-roughened muscles of his chest. "He's practically mesmerizing them. How does he do it?"

"I used to wonder about that myself," Oliver said, his thoughtful gaze also on Rex. "His voice is damn good, but I've heard better. He's good-looking, but not fantastically handsome. I finally decided that it was sheer love. He's so passionately in love with his damn music!" He shrugged. "I guess the audience feels it and responds. He should never have quit performing. It was a mistake. He needs it to complete him."

"But the songs of his I've heard tonight are so incredibly beautiful," she protested. "Surely the creation of such music must give its own satisfaction."

"Maybe," he said absently. "But look at his face."

Tamara could see what Oliver meant. Rex's expression was lit from within in wild exhilaration, and he looked more vividly alive than anyone she'd ever seen. "Why did he give it up?"

"He was tired. Being a superstar can be the most demanding and confining career in the world, and he'd been at the top of the heap since he was nineteen. He'd become so popular that the personal appearances were interfering with his composing. So he just threw in the towel and swore he'd never perform again." Oliver smiled.

"I knew he'd get bored eventually. I'm surprised he lasted as long as he did."

Rex had finished his song and had risen to his feet, one arm raised to acknowledge the wild acclaim he was receiving from the audience. Tamara could almost feel the waves of emotion pouring out to surround his exultant figure. How incredibly heady to be the recipient of that overpowering adoration, she thought, awed. It would make one feel almost godlike to inspire such a response.

Then he was running lithely offstage, his face dewed with perspiration, his dark eyes blazing with excitement. He paused beside them for a brief moment, accepting the towel Oliver handed him and patting his brow. "Well, am I fantastic or not?" he asked jubilantly, with the endearing egotism of a little boy begging for praise. "Did you like me, sweetheart?"

Her lips curved in a teasing smile. "I liked you very much," she assured him indulgently. "And yes, you're utterly fantastic."

"Great!" he said. He handed the towel back to Scotty and gave her a breezy grin. "Wait until you see the second half. I've just been winding up!" He bent forward and gave her a quick kiss full on the mouth before he walked swiftly toward his dressing room.

Rex exploded into novalike brilliance the moment he stepped onstage after the intermission. He had, indeed, just been winding up during the first part of the show, Tamara thought breathlessly. He went from peak to peak and took the audience with him, until they were drunk and almost hysterical with emotion. He did three encores at the end of the show, and the roaring audience was on its feet demanding more when he raised both his arms and grinned beguilingly.

"I don't want to leave you, either," he said in a husky voice. "Will you let me sing one more song?"

The answer from the crowd probably shook the rafters of the stately old concert hall.

"Terrific," he said, as he settled back on the stool. "Because this is a very special song. It's brand new and it's for my lady."

Tamara's breath caught in her throat and she barely heard the first few chords of the guitar or the surprised murmur that ran through the auditorium.

Sweet my lady, weave your magic spell.
Bring me to your arms and let me love.

The throbbing, beautiful notes flowed out with a curious intimacy into the darkness, and Rex's face as he sang them had a sensual poignancy that was almost as moving as the song itself.

There were tears flowing down Tamara's face as the last note died away. "It's so lovely," she murmured.

"It's better than that," Oliver said, a trace of excitement in his gravelly voice. "It'll probably go platinum!"

With a wave of acknowledgement, Rex made his final exit from the stage. This time he didn't stop but continued straight down the corridor to his dressing room, surrounded by musicians and technicians eager to congratulate him. Tamara felt an odd sense of desolation as he disappeared from view.

"Well, Miss Ledford, how does it feel to have

the foremost pop composer in America write a song for you?" Oliver's voice cut caustically across the euphoric plane she'd been wafted to when Rex had announced his dedication.

But she wouldn't let Oliver's sarcasm destroy this moment. "It's the loveliest thing that's ever happened to me," she said with quiet sincerity.

There was a flicker of surprise in Oliver's gray eyes before he said, reluctantly, "If you can manage to inspire any more songs of that caliber, you may be an asset after all."

"That's very generous of you to say so," she said, her violet eyes twinkling. "Do you think I may even be worth the Lotus?"

"Rex told me you wouldn't take the car . . . or the necklace," he said gruffly. Then quickly standing up, he helped her down from the stool. "Come on, it's time we got moving. Rex is having a press conference in his dressing room, and I promised I'd deliver you when they were about ten minutes into the interview."

"Won't he be tired after the show?" she asked, accompanying Oliver obediently. "I'd think he'd be too drained to bother with the press."

"Not Rex. He's so full of adrenaline he's high as a kite after a performance."

They'd reached the dressing room and Oliver opened the door and aggressively pushed their way into the small room that was crowded with reporters. They were ignored by the press, which concentrated with single-minded attention on Rex's vital, magnetic figure, sprawled in a chair. Oliver and Tamara stood in the back of the room watching as he answered some questions and parried others good-naturedly.

Tamara was sure he hadn't noticed their presence until one reporter asked sharply, "Your last song came as quite a surprise, Rex. It's the first time you've ever dedicated a song to anyone. Who is 'my lady'?"

Rex smiled slowly. "I thought you'd ask that. Tamara!"

The crowd of reporters parted as Rex beckoned in Tamara's direction. Oh no, he wouldn't expose her to this, would he? It seemed he would. Oliver nudged her firmly in the small of her back, propelling her forward, and she reluctantly made her way to Rex's seated figure. She could feel the color flood her cheeks as he took her hand and kissed it lingeringly. "Gentlemen, this is 'my lady,' Tamara Ledford."

There was an immediate volley of questions that Rex deftly parried until one reporter queried if Tamara was an actress or in the entertainment field.

Rex's eyes lit with mischief as he continued to hold Tamara's hand firmly in his own. "I can see how you might think so," he drawled. "She's gorgeous, isn't she?" There was a murmur of laughing assent and he continued solemnly, "Actually, her occupation is slightly more bizarre. Tamara is a genuine, card-carrying witch. How else do you think she beguiled me into writing that song for her?"

There was a burst of laughter from the reporters and Tamara's embarrassment and annoyance increased tenfold. But Rex wasn't through. "I'm quite serious," he said, with a grin that belied his words. "It's the eye of newt keeping her complexion that satin smooth, and she can brew up a love potion that can lay any man low." He looked up and winked outrageously into her angry face. "She's a very dangerous lady."

Before she could make the indignant response this remark deserved, Rex quickly changed the subject and released her hand. Oliver was beside her instantly, adroitly extricating her from the crowd and out of the room. She soon found herself outside the concert hall and bustled into a taxi.

SEVEN

As they pulled away from the hall, Oliver turned to her with a frown. "Rex wanted to send you home in the limousine, but I talked him out of it. He's going to need all the protection he can get when he leaves the hall. That crowd at the stage door will tear him apart."

Tamara was still so annoyed at Rex's blatant ridicule of her before the reporters that she didn't answer. She was silently fuming during the entire drive to the apartment.

When Oliver had escorted her to the apartment door, he took a final look at her angry face and said dryly, "I have to make an appearance at a party the promoters of the concert are giving, since Rex is coming right home. You won't try to drown him again before I get back, will you?"

Her violet eyes flashed fire. "I might, Mr. Oliver. I just might!" She entered the apartment and slammed the door behind her.

She strode furiously into the bedroom, dropped the sumptuous cloak on the bed, stripped off the rest of her clothes, and stuffed her hair into a shower cap. She stepped into the shower stall and turned the water on full blast, letting the spray wash away a tiny amount of the irritation she was feeling toward Rex. What had possessed him to embarrass her in front of all those reporters, she wondered in exasperation. He'd known she preferred to keep her association with him as discreet as possible, and yet he'd deliberately made her the amused focus of the reporters from probably half a dozen newspapers.

By the time she'd finished her shower and slipped on her nightgown and tailored white satin robe, she'd worked herself into a fine state of indignation. She could hardly wait to confront Rex with her anger. After an hour's impatient pacing and aimless wandering about the living room, though, she decided to go to the kitchen and make herself that sandwich Rex had mentioned earlier.

She'd put on a pot of coffee, removed a plate of ham from the refrigerator, and was looking futilely for bread in the many walnut cabinets when Rex drawled from the doorway, "Ah, could any man ask for more? A gorgeous woman puttering happily about the kitchen and waiting for him to come home."

She threw him an icy glance. "I'm not puttering happily," she said, slamming another cabinet door. "I can't find the damn bread!"

"In the red bread-saver on the counter," he said, strolling forward and seating himself on a high stool at the scarlet serving bar. "Is that coffee I smell?" he asked wistfully. "You wouldn't want to give a poor entertainer a cup?"

"No, I would not!" she said shortly, as she drew out two slices of bread from the red metal container and proceeded to build herself a generous sandwich. "I wouldn't give you a glass of water if you were dying of thirst." She noticed with annoyance that he was still wearing the dark suede pants, and his white corsair's shirt was unbuttoned almost to the waist now. Why must the man look so devastatingly attractive?

He sighed resignedly. "I thought you were angry when you left the dressing room. What have I done now?"

She whirled to face him. "What have you done?" she sputtered incredulously. "You've only publicized our supposed relationship before the entire world, besides spouting that absurd witch balderdash and making me look utterly ridiculous!"

His lips tightened and his ebony eyes darkened stormily. "I did what I thought was best. There was no way to keep your presence in my life a secret, and I've found the best way of handling reporters is to give them a little so they won't probe too deeply. I consider that bit about your being a witch something of an inspiration. They'll be so busy writing titillating stories about my resident witch that they just may forget to check into your background."

She strode up to his stool and planted her

hands on her hips. "And what if they don't forget?" she asked belligerently. "What if one of them gets to Aunt Elizabeth?"

Rex's face clouded with answering anger. "Damn it, I did everything I could! I can't perform miracles!" He grabbed her by the arms and gave her a little shake. "Give me a break, will you?"

"That's not good enough," she bit out. "I won't have Aunt Elizabeth upset by all this!" She struggled furiously to break his iron grip on her arms. Then as her struggles proved fruitless, she gave a little cry of frustration and pushed against his chest with all her strength.

Rex's grip on her arms loosened as the high stool he was sitting on toppled backward, and he hit the floor with a bone-jarring crash!

Tamara gave a whimpering cry of horror. Rex's limp form lay motionless on the floor, his face pale and his lids closed. She dropped to her knees beside him. He was so still. Suppose he'd hit his head when he fell? Suppose she'd killed him? A quiver of shocked panic ran through her and she felt as if the bottom had dropped out of her world, leaving only dark emptiness.

She cradled his head on her lap. "No, you can't be hurt," she moaned frantically, tears pouring down her cheeks. "You're not hurt!"

A dizzying relief enveloped her as his absurdly long lashes fluttered and then his lids opened to reveal a wry flicker in the midnight dark eyes. "If you say so, sweetheart, but you could fool me," he said huskily. "Remind me not to make you really angry, will you? I don't know if I'll survive the next time."

"I'm so terribly sorry," she sobbed, hugging his head against her breasts and rocking him like a beloved child. "I didn't mean it. Are you badly hurt? Shall I call a doctor?"

He weakly shook his head. "I don't think it's anything serious," he said soothingly, rubbing his cheek in sensuous enjoyment against the soft satin covering her breasts. "It hurt like hell when I hit the floor and I think it knocked the breath out of me, but I'm in no pain right now I assure you." With obvious reluctance, he added, "I guess I'd better try to sit up and make sure."

With painstaking slowness, he levered himself to a sitting position, though not without a few muttered curses. When he was upright, there was a white line of pain about his lips. "Nothing's broken," he said, as he sank back onto her lap. "It's probably just severe bruising." He looked up into her anxious face and smiled. "I'm going to be sore as hell for a few days."

She lovingly held him and his expression became suddenly thoughtful as he took in her brimming violet eyes and quivering lips. "What can I do for you?" she asked. "Shall I try to help you get up?"

"I'm very comfortable as I am," he said, his eyes twinkling mischievously. "I wouldn't think of moving at the moment."

"My Lord, what's happened here?" Scotty Oliver roared from the kitchen doorway. His incredulous appraisal took in the overturned chair, Tamara's tear-streaked face, and Rex's supine body. He came swiftly forward and knelt beside Rex, his face almost as pale and worried as Tamara's.

Rex said casually, "We had a little accident. I

fell out of a chair. I'm okay, just a little sore. Don't fuss, Scotty."

"Fell out of a chair!" Oliver repeated skeptically. He cast one look at Tamara's flushed, guilty face and said grimly, "Well, I only asked you not to drown him." He looked back down at Rex. "We'd better get you to the emergency room."

"No way. It's nothing. Only some bruises."

"He can hardly sit up," Tamara said tremulously, smoothing Rex's shining dark hair tenderly.

"That's great, absolutely great." Oliver shook his head with disgust. "How the hell are you supposed to give a three-hour concert in Houston tomorrow night? You'll be in agony the entire time."

"I've done shows with a 104-degree fever. I can muddle through this one," Rex said stubbornly. "No hospitals!"

Oliver ran his hand through his hair distractedly. "Okay. I'll get hold of a doctor and get him to prescribe some painkillers. I guess Houston will think a doped-up Brody is better than no Brody at all."

"No!" Tamara broke in fiercely. "You're not pumping him full of drugs and pills! I'll take care of him."

"And how do you expect to accomplish that?" Oliver asked caustically. "You said yourself he could barely sit up."

"I have some herbs that will help," she answered. At Oliver's derisive snort, she added heatedly, "They were using herbs for healing and for killing pain thousands of years before modern medicine developed penicillin and Valium, and in many cases they're still a good deal healthier. I told you, I'll take care of him!"

Her arms tightened possessively around Rex, and he looked up at her with his lips twitching in amusement. "You heard her, Scotty. She'll take care of me."

Oliver gave her a black scowl. "I hope you know what you're doing, Rex."

"I have absolutely no intention of doing anything at all. I'm just going to lie here and let Tamara take care of me." He sighed contentedly.

"And I expect to enjoy every moment of it. Bring on your herbs and ointments, my lady. I'm completely at your disposal."

A frown creased Tamara's brow. "I have the ingredients to blend the liniment, but it needs heat to be really effective. Do you have a heating pad or an electric blanket?"

"Better than that," Rex replied promptly. "My bathroom has a built-in sauna. Will that do?"

She nodded, relieved. "As you say, it will be much better. Do you think you can make it to the sauna if we help you?"

He nodded. "You run along and mix up your magic ointment. Scotty can help me undress and get me into the sauna before he goes to bed."

Tamara smiled eagerly, and placing his head with tender care on the floor, leaped to her feet and hurried from the kitchen.

Her herb bag was lying beside her unpacked suitcases in a corner of the room, and she snatched it up and rifled through it quickly for the ingredients she needed. She frowned as she noticed she was low on benzoin, but perhaps if she added extra bay leaf it wouldn't matter. She hurried back to the kitchen and blended the herbs carefully, adding a bit of cooking oil she found in a cabinet, and then heated the mixture slowly over a low flame.

After pouring the warm ointment into a bowl, she grabbed several clean dish towels from a drawer and hurried quickly through Rex's bedroom into the bathroom. She'd been so furious and upset when she entered the room earlier that she hadn't noticed anything but the sunken tub. Now she realized the huge room contained not only a shower stall but also a small birch compartment that must be the sauna.

She quickly stripped off her robe and nightgown and wrapped a huge, white bath towel sarong-like about her body. Carefully balancing the bowl and towels, she opened the heavy birch door and entered, pausing just inside the door while her eyes adjusted to the dimness. The sauna was lit by a single red bulb that cast a rosy glow and she could see only dimly the benches bordering the birch walls. In the center of the room was a large metal container filled with white-hot coals and a small regulator faucet that sent waves of dry heat through the small compartment.

"Over here!" Rex called, and she followed his voice to the far side of the room. As she drew within a few feet of him, she stopped abruptly. He was lying full length on his stomach on one of the wide benches, and he was totally nude!

She supposed she should have expected it. It would obviously be more practical if she were to treat him, and she'd realized this afternoon that Rex had no inhibitions regarding nudity. It was just that it hadn't occurred to her. She allowed her gaze to trail lovingly over long, muscular legs dusted lightly with dark hair, to the tight buttocks and slim, taut waist and then up to the broad, powerful shoulders. How beautiful he was, she thought dreamily.

"Tamara?" Rex turned his head to look at her, and she came immediately to her senses. She moved forward briskly and seated herself beside him.

"I'll try not to hurt you," she said quietly, setting the towels on the floor and dipping her hand in the oily liniment.

For long, silent minutes she soothingly massaged the ointment into the muscles of his shoulders and upper back. Then she started on his lower spine and the hard, corded muscles of his buttocks. She derived an almost sensual pleasure out of the play of muscles between her fingers, and the occasional low grunt of contentment that Rex emitted when she managed to ease a particular pain.

She finally reached down for a towel to wipe her hands and said, "We'll let that ointment bake in for ten minutes and then I'll do it one more time."

His eyes opened lazily. "This bench is damnably hard," he said. "Would you hold my head on your lap?"

She drew a deep breath and felt a sudden, fluid languor in every limb. "Of course." She moved to the end of the bench and took his head on her lap.

He moved his head uncomfortably and then swiftly rolled over on his side to bury his face in her belly. "That's better," he said contentedly.

"You smell so sweet. I don't think I know that perfume."

She could feel his warm mouth move through the towel across her stomach, and she found it hard to answer. "I blend it myself," she said faintly. "It's a combination of gardenia and distilled cinnamon."

"I like it," he muttered, his teeth nibbling delicately at the soft flesh of her thigh where the towel ended.

She gave a shaky laugh. "I'm glad you approve."

He suddenly stopped his playful nibbling and turned his head to look up into her face, his dark gaze holding hers effortlessly, his face almost solemn. "It's happening, isn't it?" he asked quietly. "You're going to let me love you."

She looked down at him tenderly, noting the shadows his lashes made on his strong, masculine face. The rosy lighting turned his silky hair an even darker shade. The mint-scented heat, the intimate silence broken only by the occasional hiss of water on the hot coals, the glow that turned the room into an erotic other world, all combined to bring about a dreamy lassitude that completely banished her defenses.

"Yes, I think I am," she said huskily, leaning her head back against the birch wall.

"Tonight?"

She chuckled. "No, not tonight. You can barely move."

"Tomorrow?" His lips were once more brushing lazily against her belly and a flash of fire shot through her.

"Three days," she said firmly. "You need to rest."

He sighed. "If you think I'll be able to sleep for the next three nights, you're insane." He looked up with little-boy wistfulness. "You're sure you won't change your mind?"

"I'm sure," she said with a low laugh.

Abruptly a dark frown clouded his face. "Why now?" he asked. "Are you feeling sorry for me?"

"No, I don't feel sorry for you," she said softly.

"Then why?"

Because I love you, she thought. Because when I looked at you lying on that kitchen floor white and hurt, I knew I'd love you for the rest of my life.

"Why do you think?" she parried evasively.

His eyes danced with mischief. "Because you suddenly realized how utterly irresistible I am?"

"Right the first time." She smoothed the dark satin of his hair with a tender hand. "You've completely swept me off my feet."

"Did you like your song?" he asked lazily, his hand reaching up to toy with the tuck of the towel across her breast.

"I loved my song," she said throatily, her eyes misting. "It was the most beautiful gift anyone could ever receive."

"Well, you wouldn't take the necklace." He looked up, his dark eyes hopeful. "Will you . . . ?"

"No, I will *not* take the necklace," she said firmly.

"Oh, all right," he grumbled. "You're certainly a stubborn wench."

His toying hand suddenly gave the towel a tug that brought it slipping to her waist, baring her breasts. Tamara gave a cry of surprise. She felt his upper body rise and then looked down to watch him nip at her pink nipple.

"I guess you've noticed that I'm a breast man." Rex chuckled mischievously, and quickly suckled at one breast, while toying with the other nipple until it was a hard button beneath his fingers. She moaned, a little breathless.

His voice was hoarse and shaking as his lips left her breast and he muttered, "I'm suddenly feeling much stronger, sweetheart."

Tamara looked down into his face, which was tautened into a beautiful sensuality. He rested on his elbow. She drew a shuddering breath and, grabbing her towel, stood up. "You'll feel even better after I apply this second treatment," she said briskly. "Now roll over!"

He obediently rolled over onto his stomach, but when she pulled the towel up over her breasts again, he protested.

"Don't! I like to look at you."

She was still for a long moment, then dropped the towel and fastened it about her waist. She decided she liked him to look at her, too. She began the gentle massage of his lower back as he continued to study her.

"Not tonight?"

"Not tonight," she answered quietly, dipping her hands into the ointment again and going to work on his shoulders.

"Tamara?"

She looked up inquiringly.

"You're sure, aren't you?" he asked softly. "In three days you'll let me love you?"

She tore her eyes away from the deep intensity of his. "I'm sure."

"In three days we'll be in Las Vegas," he said thoughtfully, his eyes on her face. "I'm playing the Pagan Room at the Santa Flores, and I don't have a show the evening we arrive there."

Her hands paused an instant in their massage. Despite her acknowledgement of her desire to belong to Rex, his persistence caused her a moment of panic. Then her hands resumed their gentle kneading motion.

"In Las Vegas," she assented slowly. "At the Santa Flores."

EIGHT

TAMARA LAZILY ROLLED over on her back, adjusted her sunglasses carefully, and gazed at the exotic landscaping around the Olympic-sized pool. She sighed in contentment. The Santa Flores was a truly beautiful hotel casino, with an island motif and sumptuous air of quiet luxury that was unique in a town like Las Vegas. The penthouse apartment that had been lent to Rex by the hotel's owner was also exceptionally lovely. She was going to like it here, she thought dreamily. But then she would like it anywhere with Rex.

The last three days had passed with lightning

rapidity and, despite the mad pace set by Rex and Oliver, she'd thoroughly enjoyed them. She'd found the companionship bred by being on the road was unique and intimate and had even extended to her relationship with Scotty Oliver. If not exactly on cordial terms, they at least had developed a mutual respect which might eventually lead to friendship.

As for Rex, it seemed with the winning of her promise he'd decided he could relax, and the tempo of their relationship eased to a warm, friendly camaraderie. Not that there hadn't been moments that had sparked into near-flame. Their physical chemistry was too strong not to generate its own fireworks. She was conscious that Rex was carefully damping down the blatant sexuality that was a natural facet of his makeup, but she could still detect a virile magnetism that was very disturbing.

There had been many moments when she'd wanted to give in and tell him three days was a lifetime too long to wait. Particularly since her herbal ointment had worked so beautifully that he was almost back to normal by the end of the

Houston concert. It wasn't shyness that made her hesitate but caution. They needed the time to probe each other's minds and personalities before entering into a physical commitment she had an idea would eclipse every other facet of their relationship, at least temporarily.

Now she was glad she'd waited. She was sure her love for Rex was based on more than that magical desire he could provoke with only a long, slumbering look from those intense black eyes. The Rex Brody she had come to know in the past few days was a complex combination of tough, aggressive street kid, brilliant creative artist, and witty, cynical man of the world. Add a dash of mischievous little boy and that occasional, irresistible tenderness, and there emerged a man any woman would be proud to love. And love him she certainly did, she thought ruefully. He seemed to encompass everything she wanted in the world now, and she desired that final physical commitment as much as he. Not only for the wild pleasure she was sure he would bring to her, but for the possible bonds that pleasure might forge between them. She had less than a month to make him feel some of the love she felt for him, and she grew terrified at the thought of failure. She shook her head firmly. She wouldn't fail. She would pursue this most important goal with the same perseverance and intelligence she'd demonstrated over the years and she *would* succeed. Heaven help her, she had to.

Tamara checked her watch and noticed with satisfaction that it was almost five. Rex had asked her to meet him back in the penthouse suite at five, and then left her to go off on some mysterious business of his own. She'd decided to spend the hours until she saw him again at the pool, but it had been a long four hours. She'd grown used to being with him constantly in the past few days and she felt strangely incomplete without him.

She stood up, slipped on a royal purple beach robe over her lavender bikini, and set off eagerly for the penthouse. Using the key Rex had given her, she entered the apartment and tripped through the foyer to the living room.

"Rex," she called, "Are you—"

She stopped in the doorway, feeling as if she'd been kicked in the stomach. The woman in Rex's arms was tiny but voluptuous, with dark hair flowing almost to her waist. Dressed only in a halter top and short shorts, she was embracing Rex with an enthusiastic fervor. But no more enthusiastic than the way Rex was holding her, Tamara noticed miserably.

"Excuse me," she muttered, as the two looked up in surprise at her entrance. She ran blindly to the guest bedroom she'd been allotted, wanting only to get out of sight so she could release this agony. She slammed the door closed only to have it explode open behind her.

"Oh no you don't!" Rex growled. "I'm not having you run in here and sulk, damn it! You're coming back into the living room to meet Jenny."

"I'm quite sure you'd rather be alone with her," Tamara said huskily, not looking at him. "I'm sorry I interrupted you."

Rex ran his fingers through his dark hair distractedly. "Listen, I'm sure as hell not going to risk any misunderstandings today so I'm going to explain very carefully. That lovely person out there is your hostess, Jenny Jason. She and her husband, Steve, are not only my best friends, but I'm godfather to their son, Sean. Now will you come back and act like a civilized human being?"

Sheer relief made Tamara light-headed. "She's just a friend?" she whispered, her violet eyes starry with unshed tears.

"Scout's honor," he said, his own eyes twinkling. "Do you think I'd be crazy enough to risk *tonight* for a moment's gratification? I've barely been able to hold out for the past three days. It seemed more like three years."

"For me, too," she said, and the glowing radiance in her eyes caused him to catch his breath.

"Don't do that to me, babe," he said huskily. "We've still got a few hours to get through before I can follow up on what those pansy eyes are saying." He drew a deep breath and took her gently by the arm. "Come on and meet Jenny."

Jenny Jason was even lovelier than Tamara had first thought. She had the most magnificent, silver gray eyes Tamara had ever seen, and certainly the warmest smile. She accepted Tamara's shy apology with a friendly grin and wry grimace. "Actually, I was quite flattered," she said breezily, flopping down into a burgundy velvet armchair. "It's not often an old married woman like me is mistaken for a *femme fatale*. It was quite a boost for my ego."

"Poor old lady," Rex scoffed. "How old are you now, mermaid? Twenty-three?"

"Twenty-four," Jenny corrected indignantly. "And I'm the mother of a very hyper two-year-old, so that ought to count double." Her eyes were bright with curiosity as she appraised Tamara from the top of her head to her feet. "You're absolutely gorgeous, you know," she added approvingly. "And definitely not an Amazon."

"I beg your pardon?" Tamara asked bewilderedly.

"Rex has a positive antipathy for six-foot showgirls," Jenny explained, her silver eyes dancing. "Once one of them got hold of the key to his suite and—"

"It's an old private joke," Rex interrupted hastily, and Tamara felt a twinge of envy at the obvious long-standing intimacy between them. "Where's Steve, Jenny? Don't tell me he let you come to Vegas by yourself?"

"He's in San Francisco on business. I was with him, but I had to come back early to take Sean to the pediatrician to have his six-month checkup. After his appointment, I sent him back to the ranch with Mike and came on to the apartment to see you," Jenny explained lightly. "Steve should be back by the weekend. He said to tell you he was sorry to miss your opening tomorrow night."

Rex shrugged. "It doesn't matter," he said, his dark eyes dancing. "I'll be just as good the third night."

Jenny chuckled and glanced at Tamara. "I hope you'll work at ridding him of that terrible inferiority complex."

"Are you going back to the ranch tonight?" Rex asked, then turned to Tamara. "When Sean was born," he explained, "Steve and Jenny bought a ranch just outside Vegas. They only use the apartment occasionally now."

"To answer your question," Jenny said, "I

have a meeting at the Chamber of Commerce tomorrow morning. I'll probably be going back tomorrow evening." She lifted an inquiring brow. "Am I to have the honor of your company at dinner tonight?"

Rex shook his head. "Sorry, mermaid, we've made other plans for the evening." As Tamara would have protested, he went on quickly, "In fact, we have to get moving right away."

"Breakfast tomorrow then," Jenny insisted firmly. "Ten o'clock, and ask that nice Scotty Oliver, too."

"Yes, ma'am," Rex said meekly, sketching a salute. "It shall be as you decree, mermaid."

"Wretch," she charged fondly. Then turning to Tamara, she said, "It's quite unfair for him to whisk you away before I get to know you. We'll have to make up for it tomorrow."

"I'd like that," Tamara said earnestly. She had a notion that Jenny Jason was a person she might like very much. They said good-bye, then as the door closed behind Jenny, Rex was suddenly pulling her across the living room toward her bedroom.

"What's the hurry?"

"You have the nerve to ask me that?" Rex asked wryly. "Look, love, wear the crimson gown tonight, the one you wore that first night, okay? I have a special reason for asking."

"If you like," she said slowly.

"I like," he said, and gave her a quick kiss. "I'll meet you in the lobby in an hour."

He was waiting by the elevator when she arrived in the lobby, looking wildly handsome in a black tuxedo and white, ruffled dress shirt that only served to accent his overpowering masculinity.

"You look as lovely as I remembered," he said huskily. "Do you know that when I first saw you, you reminded me of a princess in a fairy tale?"

Her violet eyes twinkled. "So you immediately attacked me," she teased. "Not very gallant, Rex."

"Sheer self-defense," he said with a breezy grin. "Come on, princess, I have some surprises for you." He took her firmly by the arm and escorted her swiftly to the parking lot to his rented yellow Ferrari.

An hour later they pulled up before a gracious, rambling building that could have passed for an English manor house. Set incongruously in the desert, it was still very impressive.

"The Lennox Inn?" she asked, arching an eyebrow quizzically, as Rex helped her carefully out of the car and tossed the keys to a waiting, liveried bellhop.

"You can find anything in Las Vegas if you look hard enough," Rex said, grinning.

The lobby was carpeted in rich crimson and the decor was strictly out of the eighteenth century. Expecting to go through the lobby to the dining room, she was surprised when Rex led her up a stately staircase to a carved oak door on the second floor. Taking a key from his pocket, he opened the door and gestured with a flourish.

"For my lady," he announced grandly, bowing gracefully and stepping aside for her to enter. There was a mischievous grin on his face and his dark eyes were dancing.

"I think I've just stepped into the pages of *Tom*

Jones," Tamara said faintly, walking to the center of the room and looking around bemusedly.

The octagon-shaped chamber was straight out of the romantic past. A fire blazed in a huge fireplace at the far end of the room. It was for romantic effect obviously and made possible by the labor of a powerful air-conditioning system. A white shag area rug covered a vast amount of gleaming oak floor. Three shallow steps led to a massive canopy bed draped in a delicate, rose and cream tapestry print. There were flowers everywhere and of every description. There was a particularly lovely bouquet of lilacs in a graceful copper vase in the Sheraton commode; the heady fragrance pervaded the room.

Rex followed her inside and shut the door, leaning against it indolently while he watched her with a curious tenderness. "I wanted my lady from another century to feel at home," he said softly. He straightened and moved forward, encircling her with his arms and bringing her gently into his embrace. "Just as I want you to feel you've come home when you lie in my arms tonight."

"Oh, I will. I will," she promised fervently. Her own arms wrapped tightly around his lean waist and she struggled to fight back tears at this extravagantly touching gesture.

A shudder rippled through his body as she pressed her soft curves against him. He put her firmly from him. "I've planned a terrific dinner that has an excellent chance of never being eaten if you don't get away from me, babe."

"I'm not really hungry," she whispered, watching the flickering firelight play on the hard contours of his face, highlighting especially the beauty of his sensual mouth.

"Get thee behind me, Satan," he quoted thickly. He moved purposely away from her. "Room service will be here any minute. Why don't you go into the dressing room and change. I'd like to wash up myself."

"Is there a sunken tub in the bathroom?" she asked with a twinkle.

"No." He walked to a door to the left of the massive bed. "But you can order a hip bath built for two to be set before the fireplace." He paused at the door and winked. "I left orders for that to be delivered *after* dinner."

"Rex!"

Ten minutes later she stood in front of an oval, full-length mirror and gazed at a woman who might well have stepped from the past. There had been no nightgown hanging in the small closet. The only garment Rex had provided was a long, full robe of rich, creamy satin that buttoned down the front. It had long, flowing sleeves and bared her golden shoulders, only hinting at the curves beneath. She felt as romantically lovely as a bride on her wedding night.

When Rex first saw her, his ebony eyes blazed with sudden feeling and he moved across the room impulsively. He'd removed the tuxedo jacket and his ruffled shirt was unbuttoned almost to the waist. Tamara felt a sudden longing to reach out and run her hands caressingly over that muscular, hair-roughened chest, but she didn't get the opportunity.

Rex swiftly gathered her hands to his lips and, one at a time, kissed the fingers lingeringly. "'She doth teach the torch to burn bright,'" he quoted huskily, then grinned mischievously. "*Romeo and Juliet*. I memorized that bit especially for tonight."

Tamara shook her head bemusedly. He was as changeable as a chameleon. Would she ever be able to predict the directions that Rex's quicksilver personality might take?

"You're impossible," she said, chuckling.

"Impossibly hungry," he returned promptly, turning her toward a damask-covered candlelit table in the center of the room. "Let us feed the inner man, princess."

Afterward Tamara could never remember what was said over that candlelit table, nor a morsel of what they ate. Her only memory was of sudden, breathless silences, smoky dark eyes, and a low baritone chuckle that sent shivers down her spine.

After the table had been removed, Rex threw down two enormous, scarlet-tasseled pillows before the fire, and dropped down on the shaggy white rug. She came like a homing pigeon when he stretched out his arms invitingly, and he settled her beside him, spreading the shimmering blue black of her hair on the scarlet pillow. He poured her a glass of red wine from the bottle beside him and cuddled her close, fitting her cheek into his shoulder.

"Do you like your surprise?" he asked, stroking her silky hair gently.

"It is lovely," she answered contentedly, watching the light of the fire turn the wine in her crystal glass to a glowing ruby.

"I wanted it to be perfect for you," he said gravely. "No, that's not quite true. I wanted it to be perfect for both of us." He chuckled deep in his chest. "But I'm finding my patience is running out very quickly. Do you really want that wine?"

She went breathlessly still. "I never really cared for the taste of wine."

"Thank the Lord!" he said fervently, taking her goblet and placing it carefully with his own on a silver tray. Then he bent over her, his dark eyes blazing hotly. "I've been very patient, for me. Now, sweetheart?"

"Now." She barely had time to murmur the word before his lips closed on hers in a kiss that seared through her like a lightning bolt. His hard body pressed down on her with hot urgency as Rex began to unleash his pent-up desire.

"Lord, you're so soft." He groaned. "I want to bury myself in you and never come out! Touch me, love."

Her hands reached out tentatively to stroke his solid muscular chest, then began an eager caressing motion. She loved the firm, masculine feel of him, she thought, excitement turning her eyes to deep purple. She began to rake her nails lightly over his hard nipples.

Rex's hands were busy with the multitude of buttons that closed her cream satin robe and when the last one was vanquished, he opened the robe wide, revealing her gold-silk beauty in the firelight.

The expression in his eyes deepened to a glazed intensity as he rubbed a gentle hand over her firm belly. "I wish I'd saved that line from *Romeo and Juliet*," he said thickly. "You're a miracle, sweetheart."

"So are you," she murmured, as he stripped the white shirt off and threw it carelessly aside.

He was all clean, bronze lines and compact, glowing muscle in the firelight. His lean face was taut with need as his head bent slowly to take one hard nipple in his mouth.

Then, with an almost guttural cry, he fell on her, kneading and caressing her breasts with eager hands, while he bit and teased at her engorged nipples with teeth and tongue. His tormenting lips moved down to the smooth curve of her belly, and he tongued her navel with light, sensuous strokes until she was shuddering and writhing beneath him, arching to meet that teasing tongue and running her hands feverishly over his back and shoulders.

With a low groan of frustration, Rex gathered her in his arms and strode swiftly to the canopied bed, laying her down on the delicate rose and cream of the coverlet. She held her arms out to him yearningly, but he shook his head. "Not yet, sweetheart," he said huskily.

He left her for a brief moment and she heard rustling sounds as he stripped off the rest of his clothes. There was another pause and when he returned, his arms were filled with flowers. "I never imagined when I reached this particular surprise it would be so difficult to execute," he said wryly, running his gaze lingeringly over her naked golden curves and valleys. "I studied your notebook. I hope I got it all right."

He drew a golden bloom from the bouquet. "Chrysanthemum means truth." He tossed the posy onto her stomach. "Salvia—wisdom; orchid—beauty; jasmine—sensuality." With each definition he placed a flower on her body. "Lotus—eloquence." He paused as he came to the last flower, a magnificent golden iris with scarlet markings. "This one is the most appropriate at the moment. Do you remember what it means, love?" he asked, his voice trembling slightly.

She shook her head, staring up at him in bemusement.

"It means 'flame—I burn.'" He tossed the last brilliant blossom onto her breasts and then followed it down on the bed. He picked up the iris, idly stroking her breasts with its velvet petals. "Oh, yes, I definitely burn," he said thickly, and the flower was crushed between them as he kissed her shoulders and the sensitive cord of her neck before making a passionate pilgrimage to the honey sweetness of her lips.

One hair-roughened leg parted her own and while his tongue jousted and played with hers, his hips rubbed sensuously against her in an erotically intimate caress that caused her to arch frantically against his warm hardness.

"I can't wait any longer, sweetheart," he groaned. "I've got to have you!"

When he reached that final barrier, at first he couldn't believe it. "Relax, sweetheart," he said huskily. "Don't fight it. Let me love you." Then he looked down into her flushed, glowing face, her eyes darkened purple with desire, and saw absolutely no fight there . . . only a reflection of his own need. He stiffened slowly above her, and an expression of incredulous amazement crossed his face. "Good Lord," he said blankly. He instinctively made a motion of withdrawal.

"No!" Tamara gasped, her arms tightening about him. "Don't leave me."

"I'll hurt you," he said, his eyes closing and his breath coming in little gasps. "Let me go. I don't want to hurt you, love. I don't know anything about—" He suddenly broke off. "Oh Lord, I *can't* stop!" His hips surged forward and her shocked cry was drowned by his groan of savage satisfaction as he buried himself in her warmth.

He was absolutely still for a long moment, his eyes closed, an expression of almost unbelievable pleasure on his face. "So good," he said thickly. "How can anything feel this good?" He flexed suddenly and she gave a little gasp. His lids lifted slowly and he was looking down at her, his gaze smolderingly intense. "I'll make it good for you too, babe."

"I know you will," she said, smiling up at him lovingly. He felt an unfamiliar lump in his throat. "It's good now, Rex." She was telling the truth. After the first shock of pain had come this lovely stretching *fullness*.

He shook his head wonderingly. "You're easily pleased," he said raggedly, and suddenly there was that flicker of mischief that was never far away from him. "You offer no challenge to my expertise at all, love. I can see now that I'm going to have to expand your horizons." He flexed again and there was a glint of satisfaction in his eyes as a tense little shiver ran through her. "Among other things."

His hands went slowly to her breasts, pulling and pinching gently at the taut tips while he looked down at her flushed face with its expression of glazed pleasure. "Such pretty pink nipples," he said softly. "But I like them even better like this. So ruby red and begging to be suckled. Do you want my mouth on you, Tamara? Do you want to feel my tongue on those lovely nipples?"

"Oh yes," she moaned, and watched in a haze of hot, languid need as his dark head slowly lowered to her breasts. His lips brushed teasingly against her hard nipple and a ripple of heat surged through her. His tongue darted out and slowly outlined the engorged areola and she almost cried out at the tingling shock that went through her. Both of his hands reached out and closed on her breasts, cupping them.

"Fantastic," Rex breathed. His mouth suddenly enveloped one breast with a suction that was both strong and gentle. At the same time he

Iris Johansen

began to move within her in tempo with the suction of his lips. The sensation was so incredibly intense that for a moment it took her breath away.

But she couldn't remain still for long. She found she had to *move*. Her hips instinctively started to match Rex's magical rhythm with an even more explosive one of her own.

Rex lifted his head, a flush on his cheekbones and an expression of heavy sensuality on his face. "Easy, sweetheart," he said huskily. "I want to make this last a long time."

"I can't," she cried, her head thrashing from side to side on the pillow. Her hips increased their rhythm and her hands closed desperately on his shoulders. "Oh Lord, Rex, I *need* . . ."

"It's all right, babe," he crooned soothingly, his hands gently stroking the hair at her temples. "Easy now, I'll give you everything you need."

And he did. His movements took on a fiery, forceful rhythm that snatched her breath away and caused her to arch into his thrusts with an answering tension that mounted by the second.

Her nails bit into his shoulders as she strived desperately to break that tension. "Rex, why can't . . ."

"Shh, sweetheart," he gasped, his hands reaching beneath her to cup her buttocks and draw her closer to his thrusting body. "Don't reach for it. Just let it happen."

Then it *was* happening and she cried out as her body convulsed, her legs tightening around Rex in a grateful embrace. He was still moving, she noticed dazedly, and he lifted her in a final deep thrust, then uttered a wild, guttural groan that sent an odd, primitive thrill through her.

He collapsed against her and she could feel the mad thunder of his heart as he clutched her to him. He was trembling, and his chest was moving with the harshness of his breathing. Her arms closed around him with an age-old instinctive protectiveness.

It seemed like a long time before he stirred against her. He raised his head to look down at her, his dark face curiously enigmatic. Then he was abruptly rolling over and sitting up. "Stay there," he ordered as he swung his legs off the bed and got to his feet. "I'll be right back."

She couldn't have moved if she'd tried, Tamara thought wryly. Every muscle in her body felt like warm butter, yet there was an incompleteness, an emptiness she'd never known before. Would it always be like this now when she wasn't a part of Rex?

He returned carrying a moist washcloth and sat down beside her on the bed. "Spread your legs, love." Then he was gently wiping her thighs and between her legs. "Are you sore?" he asked, frowning.

The warm, damp cloth was deliciously soothing and the tenderness in Rex's face as he performed that intimate service was almost unbearably moving. "Not at all," she assured him softly.

He tossed the cloth aside and one hard, warm hand immediately began to massage the tight, black curls he'd just cleansed. "You're so pretty," he whispered wonderingly. "You're like an ebony velvet orchid with a lovely pink heart." His fingers touched that heart with gossamer-light tenderness. "So pretty."

Tamara inhaled sharply. "Come up to me, Rex," she murmured. "I want to hold you."

"Now there's crystal dew on my exquisite orchid," he murmured, his eyes still caressing her. "Do you know how it makes me feel to know I can make you do that?"

"Rex, please!"

He pulled his gaze away from her with obvious effort and shook his head as if to clear it. A deep shudder rippled through his body. "No!" He stood up abruptly and moved hurriedly away from the bed. He'd forgotten the three steps leading up to the canopy bed and she heard a small thud as he fell to his knees on the hard oak floor.

Tamara sat up, bewildered by the sudden change from passionate togetherness to this chilling loneliness. "Rex," she called hesitantly, then heard his furious cursing as he pulled on his clothes. "Rex, what is it? What's wrong?"

Then he was back at the bed, tossing her the

cream satin robe that he'd removed so hurriedly only a short time before. "Put it on," he said. "I won't have you lying there teasing the hell out of me as we talk."

She gazed at him in bewilderment as she obediently slipped on the robe and buttoned the first few buttons. She ran her fingers distractedly through her hair and the motion pulled the satin material taut over her breasts, causing him to start muttering obscenities again.

He plopped down on the bed and fixed dark, accusing eyes on her. "You were a virgin."

She nodded slowly, her gaze fastened on his scowling face. "Yes."

"Why the hell didn't you tell me? Don't you think I had a right to know?" he asked tightly.

She shook her head helplessly. "I didn't think it was that important."

"Not important? Tamara, damn it, it's important," he growled. "What about Todd Jamison and all those other guys he told me about? What about Walter Bettencourt?"

Tamara couldn't understand why he was so

upset. With one finger tracing idle patterns on the tapestry spread, she haltingly told him the truth of the lies that had been spread about her.

The explanation didn't appear to lessen Rex's ire. "That's great, absolutely great," he muttered with profound disgust. "Not only a virgin, but a victim as well."

She felt a shiver of pain run through her at the roughness of his tone. "I don't know why you're so angry," she said huskily. "What difference does it make if I was a virgin?"

"It makes a hell of a lot of difference! I've never had a virgin before."

"And I've never had a lover before," she retorted. "You're not making sense. Why does it even matter?"

"Because it's a heavy responsibility, damn it! What if I'd done something to turn you off for good? And what's more it's clear now that you've let yourself be *so* hurt by Jamison and those small-town tattle-mongers that you've kept all that warmth and passion in deep freeze for years." He ran his hand through his hair. "For heaven's sake, I didn't even protect you! I didn't think it would be necessary."

"But I *wanted* you to make love to me," Tamara protested, and two crystal tears flowed slowly down her cheeks.

Rex jumped off the bed like a scalded cat. "Don't do that!" he growled fiercely. "You know damn well what that does to me. In two seconds I'll have you in my arms, and in ten seconds you'll be in exactly the same position you were in ten minutes ago!"

"I don't see what would be so bad about that," she said huskily, her gaze running lovingly over his wide, muscular shoulders under the open white shirt.

"And you can cut that out, too!" he barked, starting to button the shirt hurriedly. "I'm not about to seduce you until I get my head straight. I've got to think."

Tamara watched in incredulous dismay as he stepped into his shoes, grabbed his jacket, and strode swiftly to the door. "I'm taking another room for the night," he said. "I'll meet you tomorrow in the lobby at eight." The door slammed behind him.

Tamara slowly sat up and automatically began fastening the remaining buttons on the satin robe. Her mind was in a turmoil as she tried to fathom Rex's violent reaction to her untouched state. She'd heard that some men didn't like to initiate an inexperienced woman, but she hadn't thought that Rex would be so prejudiced. There was a sharp ache that was beginning to pierce the confusion that beset her. Being made love to by Rex was like being on a thrilling roller-coaster ride, but it had suddenly plunged off the track into emptiness.

It had all been so beautiful, she thought miserably. Her hand brushed against the delicate blossoms that had been crushed between their eager bodies. Such a touching gesture, and so like the extravagant boy-man that was Rex Brody. She picked up the jasmine, remembering tenderly the lovely meanings Rex had intoned as he had cast the various blooms over her like a scented, velvet blanket.

She sniffed the jasmine's delicate fragrance and

suddenly felt a stabbing pain run through her as she realized why Rex had left. Her hand went lifeless and the flower fluttered onto her lap as once more the tears began to fall. He'd said making love to her was a "responsibility," but she hadn't understood. She'd taken the statement at face value and thought he just didn't want to risk hurting her in any way. But of course that wasn't the real reason at all. He'd thought she would look upon the yielding of her virginity as a commitment, having no way to know that she'd already committed herself to him totally the moment she realized she loved him. He'd been horrified at even the possibility that she might become pregnant from their union tonight.

He'd made it crystal clear what he wanted from her and hadn't put love or affection on the list. That was why he'd left so abruptly when he'd thought he might get more than he bargained for. Rex wanted no complications in his relationship with her, and he'd been careful to tell her so in a language he'd known she'd understand.

Tamara lay back on the pillow, picking up the golden iris and cradling it against her tear-washed cheek.

A jasmine for sensuality, an orchid for beauty, but no red rose for love. No red roses.

Nine

Promptly at eight the next morning she met Rex in the lobby of the hotel. He greeted her tersely and escorted her directly to the car, and they got under way immediately. By the look of the shadows under his eyes he'd had just as little sleep as she, she thought with fleeting satisfaction.

She herself had not gotten to sleep until almost dawn, but the restless night had accomplished one thing. It had formed a hard shell against the hurt and humiliation of Rex's desertion, and even produced a bit of anger to bolster the pride that had been submerged beneath her love and pain.

She carelessly tossed into the backseat the neatly folded, cream satin bundle she'd been carrying. "It's really a lovely robe," she said coolly. "It's a pity I had nothing else to wear or you could get your money back."

He glared at her furiously. "You know damn well I don't want that back," he grated between clenched teeth. "It belongs to you."

"Then you might as well give it to Goodwill," she said. "I certainly don't want to see it again."

He glowered at her. "I see you're in your usual sweet good humor. I'd suggest you temper that sarcasm a bit. I had a helluva night and you'll find I'm as testy as a bear with a sore tooth."

He had a bad night! "I can't tell you how sorry that makes me," she retorted in a saccharine tone of voice.

His hands tightened on the steering wheel, and he gave the appearance of counting silently. "Look, I'd really prefer not to pull the car over and break that lovely neck of yours," he said in a conversational tone. "So will you please shut up!"

She gave him a lethal glare and turned huffily away to stare blindly out the window. There was an icy silence for the remainder of the trip.

When they arrived at the apartment, Tamara stalked regally to the guest room and slammed the door decisively. She leaned wearily against it for a moment before walking stiffly to the center of the room and unzipping the crimson gown. It looked sadly garish in the bright morning sunlight. She wished she could just climb into that lovely, turquoise-covered bed and bury her head beneath the covers, as she'd done when something had upset her as a small child.

Sometimes it was a wearisome task to act the civilized adult and do what was expected. At the moment she wanted nothing less than to change and show up at breakfast with Jenny Jason. She had an idea those wise gray eyes saw far too much, and Tamara felt infinitely vulnerable this morning.

Well, she couldn't offend a hostess as gracious and friendly as Jenny. She stripped quickly, ducked in and out of the shower in minutes, brushed her teeth, and slipped on tailored navy slacks and an Anne Klein silk blouse with navy trim that looked vaguely nautical. She restrained her hair in a knot on the top of her head, and used a bit more makeup than usual to mask the violet shadows under her eyes.

Rex, Scotty, and Jenny Jason were already in the breakfast room when she arrived, and she slipped into the only vacant chair with a murmured, "Good morning."

Jenny smiled warmly. "You look fantastic in that outfit, Tamara. I wish I had your height. If I put on anything even faintly sailor-ish, I look like Popeye. Will you have coffee or hot chocolate?"

"Coffee, please," she answered, casting a wary glance at Brody and Oliver, who were engaged in a low-voiced exchange. She accepted the coffee Jenny handed her, added cream, and sipped the hot brew gingerly.

Jenny was gazing at her with eager silver eyes. "Look, Tamara, why don't you go with me to this Chamber of Commerce meeting? Then we can have lunch and maybe do some shopping later. I'd really like to get to know you better." She made a face at Rex. "He'll probably be rehearsing most of the afternoon, so it will be the perfect time."

"I'd like that," Tamara answered slowly. Not only would she like to get to know Jenny Jason, but the activity might keep her from brooding.

"Good!" Jenny said briskly. "Now let's get breakfast over with so we can get going." She gestured to the silver-covered trays on the table. "It's standard hotel fare, I'm afraid. When we moved to the ranch our cook, Mike Novacek, went with us." Her eyes twinkled. "He'd just married a Las Vegas showgirl and I think he was afraid to leave her here in temptation's way."

Oliver looked up abruptly, breaking off his conversation with Rex. "You received a letter yesterday in care of Rex," he said to Tamara, pulling an envelope out of his pocket. "I meant to give it to you, but I didn't get the chance."

"Thank you," Tamara said absently. "It must be from Aunt Elizabeth." But when she opened the envelope, there was an engraved invitation inside. A puzzled frown creased her brow and then she started to chuckle. "It's got to be some kind of joke," she murmured, shaking her head ruefully.

"What is it?" Jenny asked curiously, and even Rex looked up.

"I'm officially invited to be a guest of honor at a meeting of a witches' coven," Tamara said, grinning. "It's being held tonight at midnight in some ghost town by a local Las Vegas coven."

"How exciting!" Jenny exclaimed. "Which ghost town?"

Tamara looked down at the invitation. "Lucky Creek. What a peculiar name."

"I adore ghost towns," Jenny said dreamily. "We gave our first-anniversary party in a ghost town called Caleb's Gulch. It was a wonderful celebration, wasn't it, Rex?"

There was a glint of tenderness in Rex's eyes as he gazed at Jenny's glowing face. "It was a great party, mermaid. Steve really threw a wingding."

Tamara felt a twinge of envy at the gentleness in Rex's voice. It seemed a long time since she'd been the recipient of anything but scowls and sarcasm from him.

She put down the invitation. "Well, it's obviously someone's idea of a practical joke," she said carelessly. She helped herself to a piece of toast from a serving tray.

"I'm not so sure," Jenny said thoughtfully. "I read somewhere that there are really hundreds of covens all over the country. Some of them are the real thing and some just play at it for kicks."

"But why me?"

"Why, that newspaper story, of course," Jenny answered promptly. "They must have seen your picture and decided you'd be a star attraction at their little affair."

Rex muttered something under his breath that sounded like a shocking obscenity.

"What newspaper story?" Tamara asked carefully.

"Haven't you seen it? I picked up a copy at a drugstore in San Francisco yesterday. I usually don't buy those scandal sheets, but I saw Rex's name and thought I'd see what was up." Jenny pushed back her chair. "I'll go get it."

Tamara glared at Rex and Oliver, who both looked distinctly uncomfortable. "I gather this is no surprise to either of you?" she asked.

Oliver shook his head. "We saw it day before yesterday. Rex decided it would just upset you so we didn't show it to you."

"How considerate of Rex," she said between clenched teeth.

"The article was already on the streets and there was nothing anyone could do about it," Rex said, scowling. "Your seeing it would have accomplished nothing."

Jenny came hurrying back and handed the paper to Tamara before resuming her seat. "The picture is rather good of you," she said cheerfully. "Of course, the story itself is pure hogwash."

Tamara scanned the story hurriedly. "Oh no," she moaned. The scandal sheet had made her out to be a sort of benevolent white witch, casting spells and drawing up horoscopes. She read on hurriedly. They'd even brought in Aunt Elizabeth's psychic reputation in Somerset. How had they found out about that?

"I've got to phone Aunt Elizabeth," she said, scrambling to her feet.

"There's an extension in the hall," Jenny told her.

There was no answer at Aunt Elizabeth's, which only increased her worry. When she resumed her seat at the breakfast table, she distractedly pushed back her plate. "There's no answer," she said briefly, as she picked up her coffee cup. "I'll have to try later."

"There were just three lines in the article about your aunt, Tamara," Rex reminded her softly. The gentleness she'd yearned for was in his eyes, but she was in no mood for it now.

"There wouldn't have been anything at all if you hadn't given out that crazy story," she said, glaring at him. "If you've hurt Aunt Elizabeth, I'll murder you, Rex Brody!"

"You're jumping to conclusions," he said, frowning. "You don't know if she's even seen it yet."

Jenny looked from one belligerent face to another and hastily rose to her feet. "If you don't want any more breakfast, Tamara, why don't we get on our way?" She turned to Rex. "If I don't see you before I leave for the ranch, break a leg tonight."

"Thanks, Jenny," he said, kissing her on the cheek. He turned a flinty stare on Tamara. "I'll see *you* at dinner," he said commandingly.

Before Tamara could form a fittingly indignant answer to this arrogance, Jenny had whisked her from the room. Five minutes later they'd left the apartment and were on their way down to the carpark and Jenny's cream-colored Mercedes.

The next few hours cemented a friendship between the two women. After the brief civic meeting, Jenny took Tamara to her favorite tearoom for lunch. They became so involved in exploring their mutual interests and backgrounds they never did make the proposed shopping expedition.

After their third cup of coffee, Jenny leaned back in her chair and made a confession in her usual frank manner. "You know, I was quite prepared to detest you when Rex called and asked permission to bring a guest with him to stay at the apartment. He'd never brought a woman with him before, and after I saw that story in the newspaper I was sure some vamp had gotten her claws into him." She grinned sheepishly. "Rex is very special to Steve and me. That's the real reason I came back early from San Francisco. I wanted to protect him from your evil wiles."

Tamara shook her head. "Rex is quite able to take care of himself from what I've seen," she said dryly.

Jenny lifted a skeptical brow. "Rex has a soft streak where his friends are concerned. He's fantastically loyal; he'd walk on hot coals to help a friend. I thought perhaps you'd managed to tap that core of loyalty."

"Well, you needn't worry. I'm not about to try to shear your little lamb," Tamara replied. On the contrary, she thought miserably, she was the one that had been left unhappy and vulnerable by their relationship to date.

"Oh, I knew that the minute I saw your face when you caught me in Rex's arms yesterday," Jenny said serenely. "I never saw anyone so shocked or heartbroken. I was quite relieved." Her eyes grew serious as she continued. "The real reason I wanted to get you alone was I wanted to explain something about Rex. I couldn't help but notice you were at each other's throats this morning, and I know the reason is none of my business." She looked down at her coffee thoughtfully. "Sometimes Rex can be very defensive. He had a childhood that would have permanently scarred most people—a mother who drank herself to death when he was thirteen, a father who deserted him and left him to fend for himself on the streets. His Aunt Margaret is the only one who ever displayed any family affection for him, and she didn't appear on the scene until after his father died when Rex was sixteen. It's a wonder that Rex lets anyone close to him. I just wanted to ask you to try to be patient with him."

Tamara's lips twisted wryly. "At the moment that request borders on the impossible."

Jenny sighed. "Well, I tried." She changed the subject briskly. "Are you going to Rex's opening show tonight?"

Tamara's lips tightened and her violet eyes clouded stormily as she remembered Rex's dictatorial demand that she join him for dinner. "I most certainly am not," she said tersely.

Jenny eyed her shrewdly. "Nor are you going to show up for dinner." It was a statement, not a question.

Tamara shook her head.

"I didn't think so," Jenny said, her eyes dancing. "Rex *was* a bit autocratic. May I suggest an alternate plan for the evening?"

"Be my guest," Tamara answered promptly. There was no way she wanted to be alone today. Between worrying about Aunt Elizabeth, and her depression and annoyance with Rex, she needed Jenny's cheerful presence as a bulwark.

Jenny's silver eyes were eager with excitement as she leaned forward. "Let's go to Lucky Creek tonight."

Tamara stared in surprise. "To that kooky witches' coven? But that was just a practical joke."

"But what if it wasn't?" Jenny asked excitedly. "Wouldn't you like to get a peek at a real witches' coven? And ghost towns are fascinating places, Tamara. That alone would be worth the drive."

Tamara frowned doubtfully. "I don't know if I like the idea of surprising a bunch of weirdos in a deserted ghost town."

"Oh, we wouldn't let them see us. We'd just take a peek at what was going on and then leave."

Why not? Maybe it *would* be interesting, and Tamara couldn't find it in her heart to disappoint Jenny. The other woman's face was as radiant as that of a child expecting a birthday treat.

"What time do you think we should leave?" she asked indulgently.

"First we'll go back to the apartment and check the location of Lucky Creek and see how far it is," Jenny said briskly. "Steve gave me a map that lists all of Nevada's ghost towns."

The following hours flew by on wings supplied by one Jenny Jason, who proved a dynamo of activity. After discovering to her pleased surprise that Lucky Creek was only about fifteen miles from her ranch, she'd insisted on Tamara leaving with her immediately for her home and spending the evening there before they began their witch hunt. After Tamara complied with Jenny's imperious order that she change to jeans and a black shirt for their midnight jaunt, they set out for Jenny's ranch.

The Jason ranch house was a gem of a Spanish hacienda with a rambling white stucco façade. Exquisite wrought iron grillwork fronted the windows and there was a beautiful courtyard, complete with a graceful fountain. The interior was just as lovely, furnished in beauty and comfort, but still retaining a warm, glowing hominess. Or perhaps the glow was provided by Jenny and the inhabitants of the gracious hacienda, Tamara thought, with a touch of wistfulness.

That evening she enjoyed a magnificent meal provided by Jenny's cook, Mike Novacek, who seemed to be more family than employee. She even met Mike's wife, Connie, a sandy-haired beauty with a superb figure and the warmth and gentleness that seemed to be inherent in the people living in this wonderful house. Connie was acting as nanny for Jenny's son, Sean, and was utterly besotted with the two-year-old pixie.

Tamara could readily see why when she met the young heir. His golden hair, silver eyes, and smile that would melt an iceberg made her his immediate slave.

It was eleven-thirty when Tamara and Jenny left the ranch and almost midnight before they reached the outskirts of Lucky Creek. Tamara's apprehension had been growing by leaps and bounds during the drive.

As Jenny parked the Mercedes in a grove of cottonwoods a little distance from the town itself, Tamara ventured a tentative comment. "It looks deserted. Perhaps it was just a practical joke after all."

Jenny shook her head, her silver eyes shining with excitement as they searched the deserted streets and ramshackle wooden buildings for signs of life. "I'm sure it was legitimate. Don't be discouraged. A coven wouldn't exactly advertise its presence. It's not their style. We'll just have to do some reconnoitering until we find where they're meeting." She quickly jumped out of the car and set off briskly toward the main street of the ghost town.

Tamara followed more slowly, a wry smile curving her lips. Discouraged! She would have liked nothing better than to give up this little adventure and was fervently berating herself for the impulse that had led her to give in to Jenny's persuasions. This desolate and deserted place filled her with a nameless uneasiness. The dark, gaping windows seemed to be watching them as they made their way down the overgrown, rutted main street, and there was an odd aura of something waiting beyond those dark windows and boarded-up doors.

Tamara shivered uncontrollably, and Jenny glanced at her curiously. "Are you cold?" she asked. "Perhaps you'd better go back to the car and get a jacket. There's no telling how long it will take to run down our hosts at this little clambake." Jenny seemed to feel none of the chilling emanations that were plaguing Tamara, and her voice was cheerful.

Tamara shook her head and made an effort to shrug off the cold lethargy that was beginning to invade her. "I'm fine," she said lightly. "Perhaps a goose walked over my grave." She made a face. "Speaking of graveyards, this has got to be the spookiest place it's ever been my misfortune to encounter. I can't understand your fascination with ghost towns, I'm sorry to say."

"Do you find it frightening?" Jenny asked, her eyes widening in surprise. "I think these old towns are just wonderful." She gazed around with infinite satisfaction. "They have such a lovely, nostalgic atmosphere."

"I guess I'm becoming a bit imaginative," Tamara said, her violet eyes twinkling. "It goes with the territory when you've lived all your life with a psychic like Aunt Elizabeth."

They'd come almost to the end of the street without seeing any signs of life, much to Tamara's fervent relief. Perhaps a little further search and she could persuade Jenny to return to the car and leave this weird place.

"There it is!" Jenny clutched her arm suddenly and pointed to a building on their left with a broken seesaw in the front yard.

"But that's a schoolhouse," Tamara protested, with an obscure sense of shock. "And it seems as deserted as all the other buildings."

"It *was* a schoolhouse," Jenny whispered, her voice tense with excitement. "But that was over a hundred years ago. It would be ideal as a meeting place for any large group. Besides, I'm sure I saw a flicker of light at that right front window. Come on, let's see if we can get closer."

She was already moving silently toward the window and Tamara reluctantly followed her. The window was almost completely covered by a thick layer of dust and for a moment Tamara could see nothing. Then, with a chill chasing down her spine, she saw the flickering lights Jenny had mentioned.

"They must have candles," Jenny whispered in her ear. "Can you hear anything they're saying?"

Tamara shook her head. The barely distinguishable figures in the room were curiously shapeless and their voices almost entirely inaudible.

Suddenly the door opened and a large, black-robed figure stepped outside, not ten feet from where Jenny and Tamara crouched. Her heart suddenly pounding in her breast, Tamara groped for Jenny's hand and began pulling her away.

Despite her earlier excitement, Jenny showed no reluctance to leave now.

The figure had turned slightly so that his back was partially to them, and Tamara and Jenny hurried down the street as quietly as they could. By the time they could see the glimmer of the shiny, cream-colored Mercedes, they were practically running. Tamara fully expected to hear the sounds of pursuit behind them any second.

Jenny reached the driver's side of the car several yards ahead of her, and fumbled at the door while Tamara tore around the hood of the car to the passenger door.

"Ugh!" The pained masculine grunt as she rammed full steam into a hard male body sent her into a panic. Instinctively, she knotted her fist and punched with all her strength. The man's torso was iron hard, but she must have hurt him for he staggered against the side of the car. She had only a moment to feel a sense of smug satisfaction before he straightened, grabbed her by both arms, and shook her until her head flopped like a rag doll.

"You damn little idiot, what the hell do you think you're doing?"

"Rex?" she gasped unbelievingly, but there was time for no more.

They suddenly heard a shout coming from the direction of the schoolhouse. Tamara looked over her shoulder to see a number of dark figures with flickering candles, moving down the main street in their direction.

Rex swore violently and tugged open the passenger door. "Take off, Jenny," he said sharply. "I'll bring Tamara in my Ferrari. We'll meet you at the turnoff for the ranch." He slammed the door and the Mercedes took off like a Grand Prix contender.

Rex grabbed Tamara's arm and urged her into a dead run to where the yellow Ferrari was parked by the road. She could hear him cursing steadily under his breath all the way to the car, and he almost pushed her into the passenger seat before jumping in the driver's side and taking off with a screech of tires. They nearly went off the road as he made a U-turn and took off after the Mercedes.

Tamara looked back over her shoulder and her breath caught as she saw that their pursuers had reached the spot where the Ferrari had been parked just a moment before. Then the shadowy figures disappeared as the car clocked over ninety miles an hour.

With a sigh of relief she sat back in her seat. "I can't see them anymore."

"We're not home free yet," Rex said coolly. "They might decide to get their cars and chase after us."

"Do you think they will?" Tamara asked anxiously, biting her lip. The last twenty minutes had been a nightmare. Now all she wanted to do was wake up into the bright daylight of sanity.

He shrugged. "Time will tell." His foot pressed down on the accelerator and the sports car's speed increased.

They were right behind Jenny when she pulled over to the side of the road at the turnoff for the ranch. Rex halted the Ferrari and opened his door. "Stay here!" he ordered.

He crossed to Jenny's car and spoke to her for a moment, then returned to the Ferrari. Jenny's

Mercedes had already made the turn and was speeding in the direction of the ranch when Rex put his car in gear and drove back onto the road, heading in the direction of Las Vegas.

"Aren't we going to the ranch with Jenny?" Tamara asked, startled.

"No, we are not," Rex said emphatically. "I told Jenny we'd phone her from the apartment." He drew a deep breath. "Now please shut up and let me cool down. I'm on the brink of shaking you until your teeth rattle."

Tamara was about to remind him angrily that he already had when she glanced at his expression, illuminated dimly by the dashboard lights, and decided to hold her tongue. She'd never seen him so angry. His face was hard and taut with rage. There was a tiny muscle jerking in his jaw, and the dark eyes were positively blazing. She noticed he was wearing the white shirt and dark suede pants in which he usually performed. He must have left directly after the show without even stopping to change.

It was the first time since the night she'd met him that he'd shown her the tough ruthlessness beneath his easy charm; she had to admit to herself she was a little intimidated. The rest of the drive was made in silence that made Tamara distinctly uneasy.

When they entered the apartment, Rex said curtly, "Go into the living room. I'll join you after I call Jenny."

Tamara wandered into the luxurious, white-carpeted room and strolled to the bar at its far end. She was trying to decide if she really wanted anything to drink when Rex strode in. He didn't share her indecisiveness. He stalked immediately to the bar and poured himself a double.

"Is Jenny okay?" Tamara asked hesitantly. The cooling-off period Rex had mentioned evidently hadn't succeeded in improving his temper. It was clear it was still at a white-hot pitch.

He drank half the whiskey down in one swallow. "Jenny is always all right," he said, with a grimace. "It's everybody around her who goes through hell."

"That's not fair!" Tamara retorted defensively. "How did we know there would be trouble at Lucky Creek tonight? We were just going to look around a bit and then get out before anyone saw us."

He crashed his glass down on the bar. "You wandered blindly into a deserted ghost town at midnight, not knowing what creeps or weirdos you might run into! What kind of wide-eyed idiots are you?" His mouth tightened. "Or perhaps you did it deliberately. You were mad as hell with me at breakfast. Was your little jaunt a ruse to worry me half out of my mind?"

"No!" Tamara cried, shocked. "I was angry at you, but I only wanted to get away for a little while. I never intended any of this to happen. How did you know where we'd gone?"

"Elementary, my dear Watson," Rex quoted caustically. "When you didn't show at the apartment for dinner, I just thought you were still upset. It wasn't until you missed the show that I began to get worried. I went back to the apartment to look for a note and after rummaging around, I found Jenny's ghost-town map." He took another long swallow of whiskey. "You'll be pleased to know that you scared the hell out of me. You see, I'd had Scotty check out that group with the local authorities in case they tried to make a nuisance of themselves. It seems they're not a legitimate coven at all. Most of them are affluent jet-setter types out to get a few kinky thrills by having their orgies and cocaine parties under the guise of a satanic cult." He looked up, his dark gaze stabbing into her. "Do I have to tell you what they had in mind for you when they sent that invitation?"

"No," she said, feeling suddenly a little sick. Rex was right. She and Jenny had been insane to take such a terrible risk. It had all seemed so safe and amusing when Jenny had suggested it, but now she wondered how she could have been so abysmally naïve.

"Then the climax to the entire lousy evening," Rex continued silkily. "After driving hell for leather through the desert to rescue you, I arrive at the scene only to be knocked breathless by you when you run into me. To add insult to injury, you then give me a punch to the solar plexus that just about put me out of commission!"

"Oh!" Tamara guiltily covered her lips with

her hand. "I forgot about that," she said in a small voice. "I'm very sorry."

"I suppose I really should be grateful for small favors," he said. He strolled leisurely around the bar to stand before her, legs spread apart and arms folded across his chest. She'd thought when she'd first seen him in that outfit that he looked like a buccaneer. The effect was doubly intensified now by the aura of danger surrounding him. "You haven't even thanked me for that marvelous getaway."

She smiled slightly. "Thank you, Rex," she said obediently.

"You're welcome," he said tersely. He grabbed her wrist, turned, and strode across the living room, dragging her behind him.

"Wait! Where are we going?" she asked as she hurried to keep up with him.

"I'm going to let you prove how grateful you are," he said curtly as he threw open her bedroom door. "But first I'm going to put you in the shower. I make it a practice never to take to bed a woman who looks like she's been cleaning chimneys." He ran a finger down her cheek and held it up to show her the dust on it.

"It must have been when I was looking in the window of the schoolhouse," she muttered absently. Then the entire meaning of his sentence sank in. "What do you mean you're taking me to bed?" she exclaimed. "What about the commitment? What about the responsibility?"

"To hell with the responsibility," he said as he pulled her into the adjoining bathroom. "Anyone with a wicked body punch like yours can damn well take care of herself!"

He started the shower, then turned back to her. She stared at him bemusedly while he impersonally unbuttoned her black shirt and undid the front catch of her bra. He next unfastened the band that held her hair in place and the silky, dark mane tumbled over her shoulders. She was suddenly poignantly aware of the overpowering warmth and hardness of him in the confines of the bathroom. She could feel her heartbeat accelerate as he stripped her of the shirt and bra as if she were a lifeless mannequin. His face was closed and expressionless and suddenly she couldn't bear it.

His hands were on the waistband of her jeans now, and she reached out to stop him. He looked up, a frown crossing his face.

"Rex, I'll do anything you like," she said quietly, "but please, not in anger."

His face remained expressionless as he gazed into her pleading eyes. "That's up to you," he said coolly. "Persuade me."

She felt a sense of shock at the bold words, and for a moment she didn't know how to comply with his demand. Then her hands hesitantly went to his shirt and slowly started to unbutton it.

"I think you need a shower too," she said huskily. She unbuttoned the last button and took a step closer to ease it over his brawny shoulders. Her aroused nipples teased him as she worked the shirt with painstaking slowness down his arms. She heard his sharply indrawn breath and watched with mounting excitement the leaping pulse in the hollow of his bronze throat. She was suddenly enjoying this. She stepped back and swiftly stripped off her jeans and the tiny bikini panties beneath. She stepped under the shower and let the water cascade over her, but she didn't close the frosted shower door.

Rex stood staring at her as if mesmerized as the flowing water turned her hair into a glossy seal-like cap and pearled in iridescent drops on her shoulders and breasts. "Lord!" The cry broke from him with guttural violence. His face was no longer expressionless but flushed and taut with need. It took only seconds for him to shed the rest of his clothes and join her under the spray, closing the shower door after him. The narrow confines of the stall forced them in breathlessly close proximity and suddenly Tamara's boldness vanished as if it had never been.

She looked up, her eyes wide and hesitant, and met his almost blindingly intense gaze. "Rex?" She didn't know what she was entreating, but whatever it was she knew it must come from him. Everything must come from him. She stepped closer and slipped her arms about his waist and buried her face in the rough dark hair on his chest.

Suddenly she heard a rumbling chuckle beneath her ear, and his arms slid lovingly around her and pulled her to him, branding her with his hard need. "Damn it, sweetheart," he said wryly, as he wound one hand in her hair. "I stepped into this shower stall expecting to be seduced by a violet-eyed Lilith and I find a young Juliet in my arms."

She hugged him closer, relieved at the thread of tenderness running through the words. "Give a girl a chance," she said huskily. "I'm a fast learner. I only need practice."

He tilted her head back and kissed her lingeringly, his tongue licking teasingly at the drops of water beading her lips. "I intend to give you plenty of that," he said thickly. His warm tongue lazily stroked the pulse point in her throat before moving down to tease her pink-crested breasts with quickening intensity.

Then he was sliding down her body to kneel before her. "Open for me, sweetheart," he ordered hoarsely, his hands gently prying her thighs apart. "I want to come in." One hand reached behind her to cup her buttocks while the other crept between her thighs.

He pressed his head to her belly, rubbing it in a nestling motion against her softness. She gave a low moan that was more of a gasp as he began a slow teasing stroking that set her afire. It was incredibly arousing, standing there with the warm, sensuous water cascading over her breasts like gentle caressing hands, while Rex's own hands were doing these fantastic things to her lower body.

His lips were nibbling softly at her belly now, his tongue stroking her navel teasingly while his fingers kept up that torrid rhythm that was causing her to arch against him in a fever of need.

"You're dewing for me again, babe. I can feel it." He kissed her belly softly. "Lord, I'd love to see it." He chuckled. "But I don't think I'd better right now. I'm about ready to explode just from touching you."

Then he was on his feet, both hands cupping her buttocks and lifting her to his loins. She gave a strangled cry as he rubbed her with a slow, teasing rhythm against his iron-hard arousal, before clutching her to him so tightly that she gave an involuntary moan.

"Sorry, love," he gasped. His arms were shaking as he carefully put her down and pushed her away from him. "We'd better get out of here before I start demonstrating a few of the more advanced positions in the Kama Sutra. You haven't even tried the basic ones yet!"

He briskly opened the shower door and whisked her out, enveloping her in a huge, white bath towel and rubbing the rough terry cloth over her with swift, gentle hands. When she would have taken up another towel to return the favor, he shook his head ruefully, and said, "Best not, babe!" He dried himself quickly and then, picking her up with the eager boldness of a corsair claiming his plunder, carried her to the bed.

In the hours that followed, Tamara at last understood her aunt's odd remark regarding the music in Rex Brody. Every movement was a symphony as he built her responses to a feverish pitch of mindless need. His lips brushing teasing butterfly kisses on her throat and shoulders was a delicate pianissimo of sensation, his gentle nibbling on her swelling breasts and inner thighs was crescendo. And then he parted her legs to enter her and show her the mind-shattering ecstasy of the final fortissimo.

Even later, as he held her tenderly against him, cradling her still damp head in the hard hollow of his shoulder, she felt the gentle, golden notes of a passionate contentment.

"Was it really good for you, babe?" Rex's words, rumbling beneath her ear, surprised her out of her euphoric bemusement.

"You know it was." She sighed happily. "You must be one helluva lover, Rex Brody." Her index finger idly traced patterns in the springy dark hair on his chest. "Of course, I'm really too much of an amateur to judge."

"Nonsense!" He chuckled. "Your opinion is probably much more valid because you haven't had other samplings to confuse you! But you're quite right, I *am* a fantastic lover."

She looked up, knowing she would see those midnight eyes dancing with mischief. "Was it as good for you?" she asked uncertainly, suddenly worried that she'd been so bedazzled by her own pleasure she'd imagined his insatiable response.

His eyes were suspiciously bright as he looked down at her face. "Oh, babe," he said huskily. His hand lovingly traced the smooth line of her cheek. "Oh, dear heaven, babe!" And somehow his very inarticulateness was most satisfying.

Rex drew the covers up about them and then laid her head on the pillow, bending over with his arms on each side of her. His dark eyes flickering, he said hoarsely, "Rest for a bit, sweetheart. It's going to be a long athletic night." A glint of mischief appeared as he added, "And then we just might take another shower!"

TEN

IT WAS NEARLY noon when Tamara languidly opened her eyes. Bright sunlight was streaming through the delicate, gossamer white drapes at the window and Rex was sitting on the edge of the bed, dressed in a black velour robe, and gazing at her with such tender absorption that she caught her breath in wonder.

"It's rude to stare at someone when they're asleep," she reproved throatily, thinking how strong and vibrant he looked sitting there.

"I like to look at you," he said simply. He bent to kiss her gently. "I like to touch you." He nuzzled her hair. "I even like the scent of you." He drew back reluctantly. "I've ordered breakfast. Sit up, woman." He stood up and strode out the bedroom door.

She obediently sat up in the bed, tucking the sheet around her and brushing her hair away from her face. It was a little late for modesty, she thought wryly. Rex had taken great sensual pleasure in memorizing every inch of her body in those wild, passionate hours last night.

He returned and placed a covered rattan tray carefully on her lap, then removed the stainless steel covers with a flourish. "I hope everything is satisfactory, madam," he said, then spoiled the servile effect by plopping back down on the bed and taking a slice of crisp bacon from the tray.

"You're not having breakfast?" she asked, nibbling at a piece of buttered toast.

He shook his head. "I'm not really hungry and I'll be having a long business lunch with Scotty and a record company executive. They want me to record 'My Lady' on a single even before my next album comes out." He took another piece of bacon and munched it lazily. "I tried to get out of it, but Scotty said Phillips arrived in Vegas last night." He grimaced. "I'll probably be in conference up until showtime tonight."

Tamara felt a twinge of disappointment that she quickly smothered. She knew she shouldn't expect Rex to throw all commitments to the winds just because she wanted to be back in his arms. She smiled brightly. "So you're going to make 'My Lady' a star in the musical firmament?"

He returned her smile tenderly. "*My* lady is a star," he said, running his hand in a gentle caress over her dark silky hair. "Don't ever doubt that, little star."

She felt an aching lump in her throat. She would *not* cry. "Are you sure you won't have some breakfast?"

"Now that you mention it, I've suddenly discovered a voracious appetite," he said lightly. "Did you know that I have a sweet tooth?"

She shook her head warily. There was a playful devil flickering in his eyes that put her on her guard.

"Well, I do. For instance, I'm absolutely crazy about honey." He picked up the small cup of honey beside her plate. "Do you like honey, sweetheart?"

"I can take it or leave it," she said, puzzled.

"I prefer to take it," he said thickly. With one deft movement he pushed the sheet down to her waist, baring her breasts. Then, dipping his finger in the honey, he placed the tiniest drop on each taut nipple.

"Rex!" Tamara exclaimed, her eyes widening.

But his dark head was already bending down and his warm, teasing tongue was licking at the honey-tipped rosette. He was most thorough and when he finally raised his head, they were both flushed and breathless.

He reluctantly covered her to the shoulders with the sheet. "You wouldn't consider staying right in that position until I come back?" he asked wistfully.

She shook her head slowly, her lips twitching at his disappointed expression.

"I didn't think so." He sighed, then rose to his feet. "I've got to dress." He strolled lazily toward the bathroom and paused at the door to look back at her hopefully. "You wouldn't care to come and shower with me?"

"Again?" She chuckled. "I'm practically water-logged!"

"Just a thought," he said, and disappeared into the bathroom.

Tamara put aside the tray and slipped out of bed. She wandered to the closet, pulled out a sunshine yellow, crepe negligee, and slipped it on. The color exactly matched her mood as she brushed her dark hair until it shimmered with blue highlights. No makeup now, she decided. She was positively blooming.

She walked back to the breakfast tray and took a sip of coffee, then made a face. There was nothing as depressing as cold coffee. She left the bedroom and made her way to the kitchen. As she put on a fresh pot of coffee, she mentally checked out the things she could do today until it was time to dress for Rex's performance. First on the list was to try to call Aunt Elizabeth again. Then she would work on her book for a bit, and then she really must call Jenny.

The doorbell rang as she was taking down

two cups and saucers from the cabinet. As she was about to answer it, Rex called from the foyer, "I'll get it." She turned back to the counter and poured two fresh, hot cups of coffee. She was searching the refrigerator for cream when Rex walked into the kitchen, looking amazingly conservative for him in a dark blue business suit. He was carrying an enormous, white florist box.

"I called down to the florist in the lobby earlier," he said, as he handed her the box. "I was hoping they'd come sooner so I could present them in a bit more romantic setting."

Her face lit up and her violet eyes blazed radiantly with the hope his words inspired. She put the box on the kitchen table and opened it with shaking hands.

Camellias. Dozens of perfect, deliciously scented, white camellias in their bed of shining, dark green leaves. A splendidly lavish offering that would make any woman ecstatic. Not red roses.

She could feel a deadly lassitude wash over her,

banishing the euphoria that had possessed her. Why couldn't it have been red roses, she wondered dully.

"What's the matter? Don't you like them?" Rex asked sharply, his eyes on her face.

"I love them," she said huskily, staring down at the flowers blindly. "I've always liked camellias." She turned away so he wouldn't see the tears brimming in her eyes. "Would you like a cup of coffee before you leave?" She walked back to the counter.

"I don't have time. Scotty will be here to pick me up any minute," he said absently, gazing at her slender, tense back in angry puzzlement. "What the hell is wrong with you?"

"Nothing," she said quickly, adding cream to one of the coffees. With a supreme effort of will, she steadied her shaking hands, picked up the cup, and turned to face him. "I guess I won't see you until the performance tonight," she said, smiling brightly.

"That's right." He stared at her pale face and wide, empty eyes. "Damn it, Tamara, you look like I've dealt you a mortal wound. Will you tell me what's wrong, for God's sake?"

"You're imagining things. Everything is just splendid."

He gave a snort of exasperation and ran a distracted hand through his hair. "Tamara..." The doorbell rang and he muttered a very explicit curse. "Look, Tamara, I don't know what the hell is wrong, but I know there's something. I'll get to the bottom of it tonight."

He strode out of the room and with relief Tamara sagged weakly against the counter. She didn't think she could have stood it one more minute without breaking down if Rex had continued that ruthless probing.

She took a deep breath and straightened her shoulders. How foolish to let it hurt her so. She'd known that he didn't love her. Nothing had changed because of two passionate nights that had given them both fantastic pleasure. Even while he'd raised her to magnificent physical heights with his lovemaking, he'd never spoken one word of love. She wrapped her arms around her body as a painful shudder shook her.

But she loved him so much. Why couldn't he love her just a little?

She walked numbly into the hall and sat down on the wine-colored, cushioned phone bench and picked up the phone. Aunt Elizabeth. She must call Aunt Elizabeth. Her fingers automatically dialed the number, and she leaned her head back wearily against the wall while the phone rang.

When Aunt Elizabeth picked up the receiver, Tamara straightened in the chair with a shock of relief. "Aunt Elizabeth? Thank heavens! I've been trying to reach you since yesterday."

"Tamara, darling, how wonderful to hear your voice," her aunt said placidly. "Lawrence and I were out in the woods yesterday, gathering specimens he wants to use in his next paper. We didn't get home until nearly ten."

Lawrence? Oh yes, Professor Billings. Tamara relaxed infinitesimally as she realized Aunt Elizabeth sounded her usual, cheerful self. Perhaps she hadn't even read that dreadful paper.

"I wondered if perhaps you'd read anything

about me in the newspapers?" she asked carefully.

"Oh yes, love. Lawrence and I have been cutting out all the stories about you and Rex and putting them in a scrapbook. Did you see that amusing one claiming you're a witch?"

Amusing? Tamara let out a sigh of relief. She should have known that sane, wise Aunt Elizabeth would never take that rubbish seriously. "You didn't mind that they mentioned you?"

"Of course not, dear. Why should I?"

"No reason," Tamara answered. "How are you, Aunt Elizabeth? What have you been doing?"

"The same old things," her aunt said vaguely. There was a short pause and then she went on briskly, "I was going to call you tomorrow anyway, darling."

"Something wrong?" Tamara asked anxiously.

"No, everything is fine, dear," Aunt Elizabeth said comfortingly. "It's just that it came in much clearer about the blood last night."

"The blood?"

"You remember, Tamara," her aunt said patiently. "I told you there was a disturbance about the blood. Well, it's the little boy's blood that's the problem. Your blood type is Rh-negative and so Rex must be Rh-positive. You must tell the doctor right away so he can rectify the problem immediately after the birth."

"What birth?"

"Your little boy's, of course. Tamara, *do* pay attention," her aunt chided.

A little boy. Rex's baby. Tamara felt a warm glow run over her, momentarily banishing the chilly lassitude of an instant before. How wonderful to have a little boy with Rex's mischievous dark eyes and sweet, loving ways.

"I'm sorry, Aunt Elizabeth," Tamara said dreamily. "I'm a little slow this morning, I guess."

"I really must hang up now, Tamara. Lawrence is waiting in the car. We're going to try the woods north of town today." There was a brief pause and then her aunt spoke again, her tone threaded with gentle raillery. "And the music, darling?"

Tamara leaned her head against the wall again and closed her eyes while two tears brimmed over and ran down her cheeks. "The music?" she echoed huskily, over the lump in her throat. "The music was utterly magnificent, Aunt Elizabeth."

"I knew it would be," her aunt said contentedly. "I really have to go now. Good-bye, Tamara."

Tamara carefully put the telephone down and walked dazedly into the living room. According to Aunt Elizabeth, she was going to have Rex's baby at some time in the future. When Rex grew tired of her, at least she would have his son. The knowledge didn't lessen her depression, but it was a light at the end of the tunnel.

She was purposely late for Rex's show that evening. She felt, in her present depressed state, that it would be more than she could endure to see him onstage when he was consciously exerting that explosive magnetism. He was lethal enough offstage.

She'd chosen a violet gown that had a romantic regency look to it. The delicate chiffon was beautifully cut to fall gracefully from an empire waist and bare her golden shoulders and upper breasts voluptuously. She had piled most of her hair in a high knot on top of her head, then brought one shining swatch forward to rest against the curve of her breast. She knew she looked well as she entered the Pagan Room and was shown to her ringside table, only a few feet from the stage.

Rex was on his last number and as usual held the audience spellbound. When he finished, everyone was standing and the applause was deafening. The house lights came up and he caught sight of her. Relief, anger, and frustration chased across his face.

He raised his hand to quiet the audience. "Just one more," he said with a flashing smile. "This one's for my lady."

Oh no, he couldn't! She wouldn't be able to stand it tonight. Not now with her emotions so raw and bleeding. She closed her eyes in pain as

the room darkened and the words came as soft
and intimate as a kiss.

Sweet my lady, come weave your magic spell.

She wished now she hadn't come at all. This
was as bad as being on a torture rack. But it got
worse. Rex stood lazily and strolled across the
stage until he was directly in front of her table.
The spotlight that followed him now included
her in its revealing glare as he knelt and sang
directly to her. She couldn't bear it. By the time
the last, throbbing notes were sounding, the
tears were running freely down her face. She was
making a perfect fool of herself in front of hundreds of people, she thought miserably. If she
didn't get out of here, she was going to fall apart
completely.

She jumped to her feet and ran through the
crowded tables toward the exit.

"Tamara!" Her name shouted over the mike
reverberated around the room, but she didn't
stop. Then she heard a woman's shrill scream of
horror and looked back.

Rex lay on the floor in front of the stage, his body ominously still. The people in the audience were suddenly milling about excitedly. Someone called out for a doctor. Good Lord, what had happened? He'd obviously leaped down from the stage to follow her. Had he lost his balance and fallen? She was suddenly running back toward the stage, frantically pushing people aside. Rex was hurt!

There was a crowd around his limp body now, and she elbowed them aside and fell to her knees beside him. "Rex!" she sobbed, anxiously feeling for a pulse in his wrist.

With lightning swiftness his other hand snaked out and grabbed her wrist as his dark eyes flicked open. "It's about time," he said grimly. He sat up and dusted off his clothes with one hand, still holding on to her with iron inflexibility. "This floor is damn hard."

She stared at him incredulously. "You were faking!"

He nodded curtly. "I knew I didn't stand a chance of catching up with you, so I decided to make you come to me."

"That's terrible!" Tamara said indignantly. "What a horrible trick."

He got to his feet, bringing her with him, and threw a warm, endearing smile to the circle of fans around them. "Sorry for the bother, folks. My lady is acting a bit crazy tonight."

There were amused chuckles from the crowd which parted as Rex headed swiftly for the door, dragging Tamara behind him. She didn't have the time or breath to protest until they were in the elevator on their way to the penthouse.

"Your grandstand play was entirely unnecessary," she said crossly. "I was just going back to the apartment."

"I couldn't take the chance," he snapped. "I wasn't about to have you running around Las Vegas in the state you were in." He didn't speak again until they were in the living room. "Sit down," he ordered.

She shook her head. "I think I'll go make some coffee. Would you like some?" Anything to avoid the painful conversation that was to come.

"You're not going anywhere until we get a few things straight," he growled. "I've been going crazy all day since I left you, and I'm not about to put up with any more of your evasions. Our relationship has had enough misunderstandings and general fireworks without your closing up on me now."

She didn't answer, and he ran his hand through his jet black hair. "It had something to do with the flowers, didn't it? You were fine until I gave you the camellias."

Her throat was so tight she couldn't speak. Her eyes were wide and pained in her pale face. She shook her head dumbly.

He was beside her in four steps, his hands grasping her shoulders and shaking her roughly. "Damn it, answer me! I can't stand this any more. What the hell was wrong with those camellias?"

"Nothing," she gasped. "They were beautiful." Then the tears were raining down her face and she almost wailed, "But they weren't red roses, damn it!"

"Red roses!" Rex's face was blank. "You put me through this hell over *roses*?"

She nodded, hiding her face in his shirt.

"You've never given me roses," she mumbled. "Everything else, but no red roses."

He went still, then pushed her away from him to look searchingly into her face. "And did you want me to give you red roses?" he asked hoarsely. His arms crushed her to him in a breathless embrace. "Good Lord, why didn't you tell me? Do you know how careful I've had to be? Have you any idea how many flower meanings have something to do with love?"

"Careful?"

"You're damn right. I was scared silly I'd frighten you off with any hint of commitment. I'd bulldozed and blackmailed you since the first evening we met. I didn't dare put any additional pressure on you. I was afraid you'd panic and run."

"I don't understand." She looked up at him bewilderedly. Her head was whirling. She'd thought she would never see the tough, aggressive Rex Brody caught in a situation that would intimidate him.

His lips twisted. "For a bright girl, you can be remarkably dense, Tamara. Do I have to spell it out for you? I could give you a roomful of red roses and it wouldn't say enough." He buried his face in her hair and said thickly, "I love you, sweetheart."

She stiffened as if she'd been struck by lightning, and he felt it. "Don't freeze up on me," he said, his lips on her ear and his arms tightening possessively. "I'm not going to rush you. Now that I've broken through that wall of reserve around you, I can wait. You don't have to marry me. Just stay with me, love." His voice was low and shaking. "I'll give you anything you want, but don't leave me. I don't think I could stand it without you now, babe."

She wanted to put her arms about him and hold him forever. She wanted to say something beautifully eloquent and meaningful that he would remember and look back on tenderly. But she was exploding with happiness inside and all she could do was try to lighten the atmosphere a little before she became completely inarticulate.

Her tone was tenderly teasing. "Will you write me another song?"

"I'll write you a symphony," he promised extravagantly, kissing her ear.

"What about that boutique on Rodeo Drive?"

"London and Paris, too. You can open a chain."

She slid her arms up to his shoulders and around his neck to toy with the thick, crisp hair at the nape of his neck. "And will you give me a baby, Rex?" she whispered.

He pushed her away a little to look down at her, his dark eyes grave. "You'll have to marry me for that, babe," he said quietly. "I know it's outdated, but I want my child to have his father's name."

She smiled up at him, and he inhaled sharply as he caught a glimpse of that starlike radiance shining out of her. "You're being so generous I think it's only fair that I make an honest man of you." She buried her head against his shoulder. "I don't want anything but you," she said with aching tenderness. "Do I have to send you red roses, too?"

"You love me?" His tone was incredulous and she had to chuckle.

"How could I help it? You've told me yourself how irresistible you are," she teased. She kissed the trip-hammer pulsebeat in his throat. "I adore you." She kissed the tip of his nose. "I idolize you." She kissed his lips with lingering sweetness. "I *love* you. Is that enough for you?"

"It may be too much," he said hoarsely, giving her back a kiss that was far more passionate than the ones he'd received. "I have a vague hunch that we should talk some more, but it had better be the shortest discussion on record. Last night was much too long ago."

She pushed him gently away and shook her head firmly. "No way. You have a few explanations to make, Rex Brody."

His dark eyes twinkled mischievously. "I was just being considerate, babe," he said innocently. "You look so warm and tousled, I thought you might like a long, soothing shower."

Soothing! Tamara felt oddly breathless as she remembered just what Rex considered a soothing shower. He was right. It had been too long and she was as hungry for him as he was for her.

"Later," she promised, with no little effort.

She released herself from the warm temptation of his embrace and backed away to perch on a stool at the bar. "How long have you loved me?"

He sighed in resignation and answered absently as his flickering gaze lingered on the silken smoothness of her shoulders. "Since that first night," he admitted. "At first I thought I just wanted to drag you into the nearest bed, but at the Bettencourts' party I knew for sure." He shook his head wryly. "It hit me like a ton of bricks when I watched you walk out of that ballroom like a martyred empress. It really threw me for a loop. I was torn between wanting to throw my cloak down for you to walk on and breaking your lovely little neck for making me feel that way." He sighed again. "And then you cried, and I knew I was really and truly lost. I had to have you any way I could get you. When I arrived at the party, I fully intended to tell you I wasn't going to pursue the matter with your aunt any further."

"What!" Tamara exclaimed, her eyes widening in shock.

He grinned sheepishly. "I had a talk with Aunt

Margaret when I got back to the house and she convinced me your aunt was innocent of any intentional wrongdoing. I'm not saying I wasn't going to continue my pursuit of you, but I was going to relinquish that particular lever."

"Your good intentions certainly didn't last long," she said tartly.

"I didn't have time," he said defensively. "I was going on tour in three days, and I wasn't about to leave you to Jamison and Hellman and all those other small-town Romeos." He scowled darkly. "I was already jealous as hell thanks to that shrew Celia Bettencourt."

"So you decided just to disrupt my entire life and make me come with you." She shook her head wonderingly. "You can be a very ruthless man, Rex."

"It was necessary," he said simply. "You were the most important thing in my life. I couldn't risk losing you. Going to bed with you wasn't going to be enough. I had to have enough time to make you feel something for me."

"Oh, I feel something," Tamara assured him

fervently, and was rewarded by a brilliantly tender smile.

"Do you know that in that violet gown your eyes are almost amethyst?" he asked inconsequentially, and she gave him a reproving frown. "Oh, all right. But I kept the necklace just in case."

Her lips went up at his little-boy stubbornness. "I'll let you give it to me for a wedding present," she said softly, her eyes twinkling. "Providing you'll still accept me in my present barren condition."

"Where's your wrap?" he asked briskly, striding swiftly over to her and lifting her down from the stool.

"What?" she asked, startled.

But he was already on his way to the door with her in tow. "Never mind, you won't need it. It's a warm evening and we'll only be gone an hour or so."

"But where are we going?" she asked breathlessly, digging in her heels at the front door.

"We're going to get married, of course," he

said nonchalantly. "There are wedding chapels open twenty-four hours a day in Las Vegas."

"But I didn't mean now," she protested. "I don't want to get married in Las Vegas! I want Aunt Elizabeth at my wedding."

He frowned. "And I want to be married tonight," he said stubbornly. "I want you to belong to me right now."

He was so like an endearingly lovable little boy who didn't want to wait for his treat that the temptation to give in was almost irresistible. She wanted him to belong totally to her now, too. But there was Aunt Elizabeth to consider. She would be so hurt if she wasn't at Tamara's wedding.

She looked at him through her long lashes and smiled demurely. "I don't want to be married like this, Rex," she pleaded softly. "Just look at me! I'm so warm and tousled." She deliberately repeated his words. "I think I definitely need a shower!"

Rex chuckled ruefully. "You've hit upon the one irrefutable argument, love." His hand reached out to cup the curve of her cheek. "Perhaps we'll wait until tomorrow, after all. I'll fly your aunt out for the wedding and we'll have the ceremony tomorrow evening. Is it a deal?"

She nodded happily and he leaned down to kiss her gently. "Besides, I've been thinking about those demands of yours, and I feel bound to honor my commitments at once." His midnight dark eyes were dancing. "The first two I can take care of fairly easily. I'll start on your symphony next week, and tomorrow I'll tell Scotty to process the purchase of those boutiques."

"But I was joking. I don't want—" she protested, but he put his hand on her lips, silencing her.

"Hush, woman, your master is speaking," he said grandly, and then uttered a surprised "Ouch" as she bit his finger. He moved his hand cautiously and continued wryly. "As I was saying, since your last request may be the most time-consuming to comply with, I think we'd better start working on it right away."

"The baby?" she whispered softly, her violet eyes suddenly lighting.

"The baby," he affirmed. He pulled her close again and kissed her with a hot, slow passion that was honey sweet. When he drew away, they were both shaking and breathless. "I find I'm growing very fond of the idea of having a miniature violet-eyed sorceress around the house," he said thickly.

She smiled serenely and tilted her eager lips to tempt his own. "You'll have to wait a bit," she said dreamily. "The first one is going to be a boy."